EMBASSY OF THE DEAD

EMBASSY OF THE DEAD

LEAVE YOUR LIFE AT THE DOOR. (THANKS.)

Will Mabbitt

With illustrations by
Chris Mould

Orion
Children's Books

ORION CHILDREN'S BOOKS

First published in Great Britain in 2018 by Hodder and Stoughton

1 3 5 7 9 10 8 6 4 2

A CIP catalogue record for this book
is available from the British Library.

ISBN 978-1-5101-0455-6

Printed and bound by CPI Group (UK) Ltd, Croydon, CR0 4YY

The paper and board used in this book are made
from wood from responsible sources.

Orion Children's Books
An imprint of
Hachette Children's Group
Part of Hodder and Stoughton
Carmelite House
50 Victoria Embankment
London EC4Y 0DZ

An Hachette UK Company
www.hachette.co.uk www.hachettechildrens.co.uk

To James

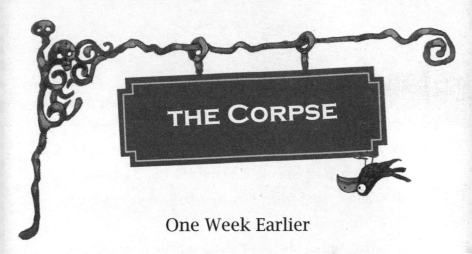

THE CORPSE

One Week Earlier

There are some things in life and death that are certain. One of those things is that a man digging a hole in the dead of night is definitely up to no good.

A lamp swung in the branches of a hawthorn tree and the shadows of the headstones jumped around the overgrown graveyard. In the silence of the hour, each thrust of the shovel seemed loud enough to wake the dead that slept for eternity beneath the cold, hard earth.

There was the unmistakable sound of metal scraping against wood. The huge man digging the hole grunted, straightened his back and wiped a grimy hand across his sweaty, sloping brow. He looked up as another figure stepped from the shadows, carefully avoiding the patches of wet mud.

This second man had done no digging. Even in the darkness that fact was clear as day. His sharply tailored suit was still in impeccable condition, unplucked by the prickles of the hawthorn trees and unsoiled by the fresh dirt that had been removed from the ground.

The suited man watched as the remains of a partly rotted coffin was manhandled from the grave. Now it sat beside the hole. He leaned forward as his brutish accomplice began to crowbar the lid open, the damp wood separating easily from the rusty nails. A satisfied smile flickered across the suited man's face at the acrid stench of embalming fluid released from within. He reached inside and lifted the corpse's hand to the lamplight.

He had found what he was looking for.

'It is you,' he whispered. 'After all this time. It is really you.'

He looked at the corpse's withered and lifeless face, then reached out to brush a strand of black hair from a cold, grey forehead.

'Your time has come at last!'

THE BOX

Jake Green was definitely alive. He was alive when he woke up, he was alive all day at school, and he was currently still alive as he trudged his way home through the little village of Elmbury. Being alive was something Jake took for granted. For as long as he could remember he had always been that way. Jake found being alive quite easy. All you needed to do was not die – and so far, for Jake, that had come naturally.

He turned to head up the dark alleyway that cut between the high flint wall and the back of a row of houses. Jake didn't normally come this way – like a lot of the living, he associated darkness with danger. But it was a shortcut, and the late-October sun was already low in the sky, and he was keen to get home.

Jake's phone bleeped. He unbuttoned the pocket of his coat and reached inside. It was a message from Sab, his best friend. If Jake was honest, the job of being his best friend wasn't a highly sought-after one, but they'd found a common interest in playing computer games and a common disinterest in studying. They had a mutual respect for each other, too. Sometimes that was all you needed. Jake opened the text.

Ready for tomorrow, idiot?

It was the sort of message that was typical of Sab. He was talking about their school trip: three days away from home. It sounded all right when you said it like that. But three days studying rock formations didn't sound quite as fun. Still, Jake was looking forward to the trip. It would be good to get away from what Sab called his 'Mum and Dad situation'. It was the only thing Sab didn't make jokes about. Sab knew what it was like. His parents had split up too. It wasn't a common interest as such. More of a shared affliction.

Given how things were at home, Jake had jumped at the chance to get away for a while. His suitcase was packed and ready to go, waiting in the spare room at his dad's place. He typed his reply:

Yup.

Then as an afterthought he added:

Idiot.

It was the little details that made their friendship work.

The phone bleeped again.

How's it going? Love you. Dad xx

Jake rolled his eyes. Dad signed all his messages like that. Like he was writing a postcard or something. As though he thought Jake wouldn't know who they were from.

To say Dad hadn't kept up with the forward progress of mobile technology was an understatement. He preferred old-fashioned things, like his campervan. In Jake's opinion, Dad buying the van was when things had started to go wrong. He typed a reply:

> You'd know if you still lived with us.

Jake's thumb hovered over the send icon, but he knew he wouldn't tap it. He returned the phone to his pocket.

There was a quiet rustling sound in the bush. Jake paused as a cat emerged from the shadows.

'Hello, cat,' said Jake. He'd always wanted a pet, but Mum was too busy to look after one, and Dad . . . well, Dad *probably* wasn't responsible enough to have a pet. Jake squatted down and reached out to stroke the cat behind the ears, but it suddenly arched its back and hissed.

'It's OK, cat . . .' he moved his hand out of scratching range, then stopped. He looked at the cat. It wasn't hissing at him. It was hissing at something behind him.

A chill swept over Jake's body. He had a strange

feeling that someone was there. Taking a deep breath, he slowly stood up and turned around.

The alleyway was empty.

He breathed out heavily. 'Stupid cat,' he muttered, turning round to continue on his way. But the words caught in his throat, hindered by the fact that he could not close his mouth.

Where once the alleyway ahead was clear, now a man, tall, thin and stooping, stood within touching distance, blocking his path.

A top hat added to his already looming height and a tattered black coat flapped behind him in a sudden, cold breeze. To Jake he seemed the very picture of what an undertaker should look like, which was a) solemn, and b) wrinkly.

The man inspected Jake through small, baggy eyes perched closely together over a beak-like nose that, along with his flapping coat and long, thin legs, gave him the appearance of some kind of sinister wading bird.

The man took a pocket watch from his waistcoat and inspected it. He frowned and placed the timepiece back into his pocket.

'Good morning,' he said in a deep voice.

Jake blinked. It was the afternoon – maybe even the evening – though he wasn't too sure where one *officially* ended and the other began. He looked up at the darkening sky. Even if it was morning, it couldn't by any stretch of the imagination be referred to as a *good* one. He didn't know how to reply and he definitely didn't want to start a conversation about the correct greeting to use when a person looms out of the shadows to surprise a child in a dark alleyway.

'Er . . . yup. Good morning,' he croaked, slowly edging backwards, tightening his frightened, sweaty grip on his phone.

The man removed his hat to reveal thinning grey hair and a wrinkled brow. He tucked the hat beneath a long arm. Some dirt fell from the brim.

'You be a little early, but I appreciate punctuality. Pleased to be making your acquaintance,' he said, not looking particularly pleased. 'The name's Stiffkey, but I'm sure you already know that.' He peered at Jake through narrowing eyes. 'I've a package for you.'

The man reached into the dark folds of his coat and retrieved a clipboard and pen that he handed to Jake. Jake stared at a form on the clipboard, his brain refusing to read what his eyes could see.

'You can just mark it with a cross,' said the man, sternly, 'if you ain't been sufficiently schooled to read or write.' He pointed a long grey finger to a space for a signature. 'Although that would be highly irregular for someone of your position.'

Jake unhooked the pen. He was standing in a dark alley with the sort of man the phrase *I wouldn't want to meet him in a dark alley* was invented for. It was probably best to skip to the end of the form as quickly as possible. He signed his name in an elaborate swirl of letters and loops that was illegible but looked cool. He'd been practising for when he eventually became famous for something. He blew on the ink and handed the clipboard back to Stiffkey.

Stiffkey looked at Jake over the top of the clipboard. 'A mere child,' he said, sighing. 'No good will come of this . . .' He shook his head slowly and replaced the clipboard in his coat. 'But no good ever comes from the living meeting the dead.'

Jake might not have put much effort into staying alive so far, but right now he was conscious of definitely wanting to remain that way. He took a cautious step backwards, preparing to run.

Stiffkey stepped forward, stooping until his eyes were inches from Jake's.

Once more he reached into the deep folds of his coat and pulled out a package – a small parcel wrapped in brown paper and tied neatly with twine. He pressed it into Jake's hands. It was surprisingly heavy. Jake blinked and looked up at Stiffkey, unsure of what to do next.

Stiffkey's mouth formed a tight smile, almost a grimace, and he breathed in deeply through his nose and then out again. 'I know you will protect the box and carry out the Embassy's orders. To be unburdened of the damned thing after all this time is a relief, I don't mind admitting it. Good luck.'

He jammed the top hat back on his head and, starting from the hands and nose and working slowly inwards, faded into nothingness, until only a neat pile of freshly dug earth remained.

Jake blinked again.

'Goodbye, Stiffkey,' he said quietly and shook his head in disbelief.

I have just seen a ghost!

THE FINGER

Mum knocked on the bathroom door. 'What are you doing in there? You're supposed to be at Dad's in ten minutes.'

Jake looked at the package. It was still unopened. 'What do you think? I'm doing a poo.' It was a panic response. He could sense Mum was still on the landing, so he noisily slid his trousers down round his ankles, sat on the toilet seat in his pants and attempted to whistle. Jake couldn't whistle. He wasn't sure why he'd even tried. It just seemed that whistling was something you should do to distract someone from thinking you were doing something else. Something you shouldn't be. On second thoughts, it was probably for the best he couldn't whistle. Mum was too smart for that kind of trick. It wasn't like she was Dad. Dad would fall for anything.

Jake sat in silence, contemplating the parcel in his hands.

Mum's voice came through the door again, 'Are you worried about the school trip?'

Jake rolled his eyes. She wasn't falling for the fake-pooing story.

He'd actually forgotten all about the trip – probably something to do with being given a mysterious box by a ghost.

Mum tried again. 'Is it. . . something else?'

He heard her sit down on the floor outside. She wasn't giving up. 'You don't have to talk about it if you don't want to, love.'

That was what she always said when she wanted to talk about *it*. *It*, by the way, was Dad moving out.

Jake still didn't reply. Instead, he turned the package over in his hands and inspected the neat wrapping.

'You know it's not your fault, don't you?' Her voice was quieter now. Like she was talking to herself.

Yeah, I know . . . It's your fault. Yours and Dad's.

He couldn't say those words aloud because it would upset his mum and that wasn't what he wanted. He just wanted everything to be the same as it was before.

'It's for the best . . .' came his mum's voice again, 'in the long term.'

The long term. That's what Mum and Dad always said. But when does the long term start? It had been four months since Dad had left and it didn't feel like that they'd reached 'the best' yet.

Mum knocked on the door. 'Jake? You know we both love you, don't you?'

Jake let out a deliberately dramatic sigh. '*Please*, Mum. Some privacy?'

There was a silence. Then the sound of Mum's footsteps walking down the stairs.

Jake shook his head, trying to clear his brain.

Earlier he had seen a ghost.

And the ghost had given him a package.

Should he open it?

Probably best not to open it.

Jake's fingers closed around the loose end of the twine that bound the parcel.

Definitely best not to open it.

It had been given to him, though.

No good ever comes from the living meeting the dead.

Jake tugged at the twine. Now the knot was undone. He slowly unwrapped the brown paper to reveal a small wooden box. He turned it round in his fingers. The box's worn and well-handled appearance gave no clue to its contents apart from a tatty label with a strange symbol inked upon it: three vertical lines crossed by three horizontal lines, like a small grid. A fine brass clasp held a hinged lid in place. Jake took a deep breath and unhooked the clasp. Carefully, he began to lift the lid.

The box was lined with a cold, greyish metal. That's why it was so heavy. Maybe it was lead, Jake thought. He seemed to remember something about lead being heavy. Inside, the box was full of strips of ancient yellowed newspaper. Perhaps they were protecting something? Cautiously, he picked the pieces out.

Jake stopped suddenly. There was something in the box.

At first he just caught a glimpse. A pale yellowy glimpse that made his stomach tighten, like he was going to vomit all over his lap.

Holding his breath, he parted the packaging further. There, cushioned on a piece of folded newspaper, was a withered and wrinkled, severed human finger.

Jake slammed the lid closed. He breathed out. Then he looked around. Even though he sat alone, trousers round ankles, in a locked bathroom, he had a funny feeling he was being watched.

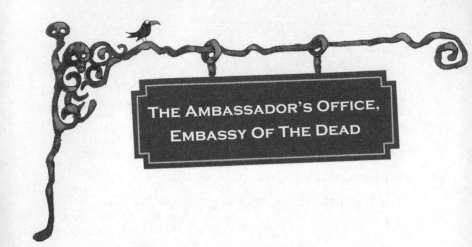

Maureen had been dead for ages now and it still amazed her that the Embassy and Afterworld was technologically so far behind the Earthly Plane. Still, it wasn't for her to worry about. Despite the frustrations of her outdated printer, and her boss's moods, Maureen enjoyed her job as Personal Assistant to the Ambassador of the Embassy of the Dead.

The light on Maureen's printer came on and the machine started to hum. A memo was coming through. She checked the paper as it emerged.

Clause 7.3 – Death Order.

She raised an eyebrow. They didn't get one of those very often. She put on her reading glasses as she waited for the report to finish printing, then ripped the paper from the machine, reading it on the way back to her desk.

ACTIVITY: Spectral container 34 opened by an unlicensed member of the living.

PERPETRATOR: Jake Green, Elmbury.

ACTION: Immediate incarceration in the Eternal Void.

Didn't people know that unlicensed opening of spectral containers was a serious matter?

Maureen opened the middle drawer of the 'Spectral Containers' filing cabinet and searched for file 34. She smiled at the soft greyish-pink cardboard cover. Of all the card colours, it was Maureen's favourite. She'd painted her downstairs loo that same colour. It was a shame such a pretty file had to contain such dark information.

She opened the file and read the front page.

Spectral Container 34

ISSUED TO: Embassy of the Dead.

CONTENTS: Highly classified.

STATUS: If compromised, enact CODE RED
procedures.

Maureen's eyebrow, already raised, rose even higher.

Highly classified? Code red?

It meant the contents of the box contained something of a highly dangerous and sensitive nature. Maureen hadn't personally dealt with a Code Red since back in 1982. She pursed her lips at the thought of what had happened *that* day. Most disagreeable for all concerned.

So, this wasn't just a serious matter. This was a *very* serious matter.

She shuddered at the thought of what would happen now. And not just at the mood it was going to put the Ambassador in. But more than that – who she would be forced to summon from the Afterworld. There was something about him that she found disturbing. Even for a reaper he was unusually grim.

She sighed and pressed a button on her desk.

'Hello, Ambassador? . . . Yes, did you see the . . . Yes, I know. Should I summon . . . ? OK, yes, right away, Ambassador.'

Maureen clicked off and pressed another button.

'Could you put me through to the Afterworld? It's Maureen from the Embassy.'

She waited for a connection. A crackling voice answered briefly, then went silent. Maureen tutted. Afterworld technology! She tried again.

'Hello?' answered a voice, clearer this time.

Maureen took a deep breath. 'Send for Mawkins.'

MUM AND DAD

J ake gazed out of the window of Mum's car as the village passed by. It was reassuring that it was all so familiar, despite what had just taken place in the alleyway. The houses looked the same. The King's Head pub looked the same. The shop looked the same. It was cold, and wet. People were still going about their everyday, boring lives.

No one knew.

Mum glanced at him. 'You've got everything packed, right? Toothbrush, shower gel . . .'

There is a severed human finger in my bag.

'. . . and you'll phone me every evening?'

There is a severed human finger in my bag.

'Don't forget to set your alarm. Remember your dad starts work early tomorrow so he won't be there to wake you.'

There is a severed human finger in my bag.

'You'll need to catch your normal bus to school. I'm sorry I couldn't rearrange my shift.'

'That's OK.' Jake remembered being quite relieved when she'd told him. He didn't really want his mum dropping him off and trying to kiss him goodbye in front of the whole class.

'You've got the number in your phone in case of any problems, OK? Jake? Have you set your alarm?'

Jake looked at his phone. 'Yes, Mum!'

He hadn't

'You must be hungry, love. I'm sure your dad's making something nice for tea. Try to eat some vegetables. You're growing. It's important.'

Jake nodded. It was weird how having a severed human finger in his bag hadn't put him off dinner.

She looked across at him again. Then she patted his leg. 'Something's up, isn't it?'

Jake's mum was a nurse. She had probably seen loads of severed fingers – although she had never specifically mentioned any. Maybe Jake should tell her about the one in his bag?

'Give him a chance, Jake.'

She was talking about Dad again. She did that sometimes. Like she thought everything Jake did was connected to the fact that she and Dad had split up.

It had taken a while for Jake to understand what 'Dad moving out' meant. He could still remember the conversation they'd had that day.

'So how long are you going for?' Jake had asked Dad. But Mum had done all the talking. Dad had spent the entire conversation looking at the ground, while Mum skipped around the question.

'You can visit him whenever you want. He's only going to be living at the farm.'

The straight answer would've been 'for ever'.

The farmer Dad worked for was letting him stay in one of his unfinished holiday bungalows until he found somewhere better.

Jake had sighed. 'Is it because of the campervan?'

Mum shook her head. 'No. Although that thing is pretty annoying.'

Jake looked out of the car window and smiled ruefully. He could remember the day Dad had bought the campervan as a 'family Christmas present' two years ago. Mum had not been impressed. Now, whenever Mum and Dad argued – which, quite frankly, was pretty often – Mum brought up the fact that Dad had let Jake drive the campervan on the road. Jake had started learning to drive ages ago on the farm tracks, sitting on Dad's lap until his feet could reach the pedals. The week before Dad had left, Jake had been allowed to drive home from the farm, with Dad in the passenger seat – it was only ten minutes or so along really quiet roads. He could still see his dad's face, beaming proudly as they pulled into the driveway.

'You're a natural, son!'

Mum had gone absolutely mad.

But she wasn't mad when they had told Jake about them splitting up. She just looked sad. Jake wasn't sure which was worse.

'It's just that sometimes people get on better when they live apart . . . And we don't want to argue any more,' she said.

That, at least, was something Jake could agree with. There wasn't much stuff Mum and Dad hadn't argued about. They argued about work, about money, about holidays. Sometimes they even argued about taking him to school.

'Is it because of *me*?' Jake had asked.

Mum had shaken her head and hugged him. Holding him until he had to push her away. Dad was still looking at the floor and Jake could remember the feeling of wanting him to say something . . . wanting him to say *anything*. Even to argue.

Anything to change what was happening.

But he didn't.

He just sat there.

That night Jake hadn't been able to sleep. He'd left his bedroom to get a glass of water from the kitchen. When he'd got to the hallway he could hear a strange noise coming from the kitchen. It was Dad crying. Jake stopped. Then, unnoticed, he crept back up to bed.

The next day Dad had loaded up the campervan with his stuff. He hardly had anything. Jake and Mum stood on the pavement as Dad climbed into the driving seat and closed the door.

He wound down the window. 'You coming along?' he'd asked Jake. 'We can take the van out.'

He looked at Mum. 'Only on the tracks, mind.'

Mum smiled and draped her arm round Jake's shoulder. 'You go if you want, love.' She winked at him. 'He'll need some help sorting out his TV.'

Jake took a deep breath. He couldn't believe it. Dad was leaving and they were talking about the TV – normal stuff – like nothing was happening. Like his family wasn't splitting up. It occurred to him that they hadn't even asked him what he thought, like he didn't have a say in whether his family stayed together or not. Why not? They were his parents as much as he was their son. That's how families work. They stay together.

Jake shook his head. 'It's all right, Dad. I've got some homework to do.' He turned and went inside the house and up to his room, where he buried his head in his pillow and cried until he had no more tears left.

WHAT ARE YOU SUPPOSED TO DO WITH A SEVERED FINGER?

As Mum pulled up at the end of the lane that led to the farm, Jake started to panic.

He still hadn't asked her about the finger.

What are you supposed to do with a severed finger?

A severed finger wasn't the sort of thing you could put in the rubbish. It wasn't the sort of thing you could keep, either. It would probably need to be buried. Maybe the person who the finger belonged to was still alive? Unsurprisingly, it wasn't a problem Jake had experienced before. It was the sort of serious problem that needed grown-up advice. The sort of problem that needed Mum. He imagined turning to Mum and saying, '*I have in my possession a severed human finger.*'

It sounded like the first sentence in a very long

conversation that would probably end with him being accused of murder and thrown in prison. The subject needed to be approached with caution . . .

He stepped out of the car and took a deep breath. 'Mum,' he said, 'do you believe in ghosts?'

'Ghosts? No, don't be daft.'

Now what? Jake tried again. But the phrase 'I have in my possession a severed human finger' caught in his throat.

Mum looked at him quizzically. 'Are you all right, Jake?'

He nodded. It was like he had lost the power of speech completely.

Mum checked her watch. 'I've got to go. Have a nice time on your trip. Be careful. Say hi to Dad.' She smiled. 'I love you.'

Jake forced a smile back and waved as she drove off, all hope of a solution disappearing with her.

Now he just had Dad to help with the finger situation.

Things looked bleak.

He turned round. Dad's bungalow looked bleak too.

He pushed open the unpainted front door.

Everything about Dad's place was depressing. Well, it had the important things – namely, a sofa and a TV – but there were none of the pointless things that adults usually put in houses, like vases and pictures. Stuff like that. Stuff that his mum's house was full of. Maybe all that pointless stuff Mum and Dad had collected together added up to something. Like a place needs a certain number of photographs, or calendars, or tea towels for it to qualify as a proper home. Even Dad's carpet was depressing, thought Jake, as he let himself in. He couldn't quite put his finger on what could possibly make a carpet depressing, but somehow his dad's carpet managed it.

At least Dad was keeping the place fairly clean. And he didn't make Jake eat any vegetables. Dinner was already on the table as Jake walked through to the kitchen – sausage, beans and fried bread.

'Don't tell Mum about the fried bread, OK?' said Dad, smiling as he ushered Jake to the table. He had those lines you get round your eyes when you smile loads.

Halfway through eating his dinner, Jake decided to try again with his 'what to do about the severed finger' problem.

'Do you believe in ghosts, Dad?' he asked.

'Ghosts?' Dad looked puzzled. They *had* been talking about whether an Olympic sprinter could outrun a hippo.

Dad chewed thoughtfully on a bit of sausage, then swallowed. 'I don't know,' he said, cutting a new bit of sausage and staring at the wall for a minute, deep in thought. Finally, he looked back at Jake and said, 'Did you know they kill more humans than snakes do?'

Jake looked up in alarm. 'Ghosts?!'

'No, silly.' Dad smiled. 'Hippos!'

Jake vacantly wiped the last of the bean juice from his plate with a piece of fried bread and popped it in his mouth.

It was clear: he was on his own.

DO YOU NEED A HAND?

Jake opened his eyes. Apart from a crack of light that shone through the half-open door to the living room, it was pitch dark. He lay motionless on his dad's sofa, his head peeking out from a sleeping bag. Something had woken him.

Something in the room.

Seconds passed.

Silence.

Still Jake didn't move. His eyes darted round as they adjusted to the darkness. He could make out shapes: the familiar outline of furniture, the glass doors that led to the farmyard. There was no one in the room. He was certain. He propped himself up on his elbow and listened.

Still silence.

I'm being stupid.

He lay back down. Tomorrow he'd wake up early before his dad went to work and show him the severed finger. Dad might not believe the ghost bit, but he'd know what to do about the finger. And everything would be OK. It was funny, but just deciding to share his secret made him feel better. So much better, in fact, that suddenly he wanted to see the finger again. One last time. To check that it hadn't all been a dream.

Jake sat up in his sleeping bag and stretched his arm over the edge of the sofa to fetch his backpack, but as his hand probed the darkness he felt something he wasn't expecting. It was a pile of dirt. He rubbed it in his fingers. It was like the fresh soil of a newly dug garden.

His hand wandered further across the depressing carpet until it came to something else.

He froze.

It was another hand.

A cold hand that faded away from his touch . . .

Jake gasped and sprang up, falling off the sofa and on to the floor, landing tangled in his twisted sleeping bag. His heart was hammering. He opened his mouth to cry out for his dad but then, in the gloom – starting from the tip of a nose, and working outwards towards the edges – a familiar long face appeared inches from his own. Sunken grey eyes stared at him. Fresh soil fell from the rim of the ghost's top hat and landed next to Jake's face.

'It'd be a kind service to me if you refrained from having a case of the screamers, boy,' said Stiffkey.

Jake nodded. He couldn't have made a sound if he'd wanted to.

Stiffkey straightened up. 'I'm afraid there's been a terrible misunderstanding.' He raised a long, thin grey finger in the air. 'Just let me explain, because I don't want to be here any more than you want me to be here.'

Even with his apologetic stoop, he must've been a good six inches taller than Dad, and his hat merged into the ceiling. He wrung his hands together. 'Now, where should I be starting?' he muttered, pacing the room. 'I suppose I'd best skip the beginning, because the beginning is nothing to do with you, or anyone else for that matter . . .' He paused and looked at Jake. 'You know I'm a ghost?'

Jake nodded.

'And you know all about ghosts?' He didn't wait for Jake to answer. 'I'll take your silence as a 'no'. Well, there's plenty more to haunting than clanking chains and fading through the walls of some fancy old house, ain't there?' He paused, pulled out his pocket watch and glanced at the clock on the wall. 'Anyway, can't stay long. The clock's ticking and though my watch be the right time now, at the moment it mattered, it wasn't.'

Jake had no idea what Stiffkey was talking about.

'And I haven't spent a lifetime and a deathtime waiting to be Undone just to have one mistake and one child spoil it. So here's the thing . . .' The ghost crouched down next to Jake and lowered his voice. 'I was given something by somebody for somebody else.'

Jake nodded, like he understood. He didn't.

'Ain't no business of yours who either of them were,' Stiffkey continued, 'and I couldn't say even if I wanted to, which I don't.'

Jake cleared his throat. 'What does "waiting to be Undone" mean?'

The ghost's voice dropped again, now to a whisper. 'It'd be of no interest to you whatsoever to know anything about being Undone, or about the Embassy of the Dead.' Stiffkey removed his top hat, seemingly as a sign of respect. More soil fell to the floor. 'Point is, we need to right what's wrong, which is why I'm here. Earlier today, when I said "good morning?" you said "yes". But you're not good morning, are you?'

Jake scratched his head. 'How can I be "good morning"? It's a polite greeting, not a person.'

Stiffkey looked cross. 'That's where you're mistaken. Good*mourning* is a person . . .' He shook his head. 'It's spelt different, like "mourning a lost child". I thought *you* was *he*. And he's been specially licensed to talk to the dead, which you have not.'

Jake smiled. 'That's funny. He's called Goodmourning and you're an undertaker. Makes sense you'd know each other.'

'An undertaker, says you? Well, ain't you observant?' The ghost fixed Jake with a

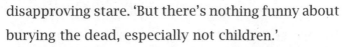

disapproving stare. 'But there's nothing funny about burying the dead, especially not children.'

'Yes, of course. Sorry.' Jake felt guilty now. Making a joke about mourning to an undertaker was possibly a little tactless – particularly if he himself were dead.

'Besides, Goodmourning ain't his true name and I ain't ever met him. It's the Undoer codename he goes by,' said Stiffkey. 'As I was trying to say, a delivery meant for Goodmourning was received by you.' He glanced around the room, looking nervous. 'So, I'm very much hoping you still have the package?'

'Yes, I've got it right here. I've not done anything with it.'

'Well, that is good news. In which case, I'll be taking it back now and we'll say no more about it . . . to anybody.'

Jake felt a surge of relief flow through his body. He was going to be free of the finger. He reached for his backpack and began to unzip it. 'And don't worry,' he said to Stiffkey, 'I haven't told anybody about the box, or about you.'

The ghost sighed deeply. 'Good. Children are the worst for keeping secrets, and though you're sensitive, you're still a child. The only thing a ghost dislikes more than a living child is a cat. Cats see everything.'

Jake thought back to the cat in the alleyway. It had seen Stiffkey before he had. 'What do you mean, I'm "sensitive"?'

'Sensitive to the ways of the dead,' explained Stiffkey. 'That's another reason I thought you were Goodmourning – you can see me, and there's not many of the living who can.'

Jake nodded, just grateful to be relieved of the burden of a severed finger. He took the box from his bag and lifted it up towards Stiffkey.

The old ghost sighed with obvious relief and wiped his forehead with the back of his hand. 'And glory be that even a living child knows not to be opening a box that bears the mark of the Embassy of the Dead!'

Jake froze. 'But I did . . .' he said.

'Did what, child?'

'I did open the box!'

Stiffkey staggered backwards. His face, already grey, turned a shade less colourful.

'But you said you hadn't done anything with it!'

'I meant I hadn't, you know, *given* it to anyone, or . . . or thrown it away . . .'

A look of horror flashed across Stiffkey's face. 'Then all is over child. The Embassy will know . . .'

'And then what?' asked Jake, looking up at the ghost nervously.

Stiffkey looked away, unable to hold Jake's gaze. 'He'll be coming for you.'

'Who will?' asked Jake quietly, swallowing. He could feel his heart rattling his ribcage.

'Mawkins,' said Stiffkey. He fixed Jake with an unblinking stare.

'Who's Mawkins?' asked Jake in a shaky voice.

A sudden wind rattled the window. Outside, a storm was brewing and a fog seemed to be drawing in around the house.

Stiffkey let out a moan. 'First the fog. Then the bonewulf will appear. Mawkins is near, boy. Leave the box here and then run . . . Run for your life!' And with those words he began to disappear.

First from the edges, until only his eyes – filled with hopelessness – were visible, and then they too faded from sight.

'Stiffkey!' hissed Jake. 'Wait!' He was frozen with panic. He knew he was in terrible danger, but he didn't know what to do. He was about to run into the hallway, when he heard the sound of the front door blowing open in the wind.

Whoever, or whatever, it was that was coming for him had arrived.

THE BONEWULF

Jake could hear something entering through the open door. Something moving in the darkness of the hallway. He stood still, listening – whatever it was, he could hear it breathing: a loud, damp, snorting rattle. Was this a bonewulf? Jake backed across the room to the glass doors that led out to the farmyard. His leg bumped against the coffee table and a mug fell to the carpet with a dull thud. He froze. The snorting had stopped. The creature, like him, was holding its breath. Listening. Waiting.

Quickly, Jake turned and tried the glass door that led to the farmyard. It was locked. He closed his eyes in dismay then opened them again in terror at the sound of something behind him. Whatever it was, he could smell it now – a rotting stench that filled his nostrils. And he could feel the warmth of its presence too. *It was in the room.*

His heart was beating so wildly, but there was only one thing he could do. Jake turned to face the creature, then immediately regretted his decision.

It was like no animal that he'd seen before. It seemed to be formed from the assembled remains of whatever dead creatures had the misfortune to have been pulled from their resting places and twisted together by some unknown force, to forge a new creature – a beast born of the dead.

Its body was made of the small bones of vermin meshed together with what smelt like rotting flesh, randomly covered with scraps of matted fur, skin, feathers. Through occasional gaps in this macabre patchwork of death, parts of the skeleton of an unknown, larger animal could be seen. An oozing, snorting, snouted, nightmare the size of a large pig – but leaner.

Set deep within its head were two unblinking yellow eyes that stared straight at Jake. This was the bonewulf.

The beast pounced and the fear that had coursed through Jake's system drained from his body. He was going to die. He felt strange – almost calm – like time was slowing down. Then came the useless memory of his mum's voice: 'Have a nice time on your trip. Be careful.'

As the bonewulf flew through the air towards him, Jake stumbled backwards against the door, shielding his face with his arms.

There was a loud clang and Jake felt something slam into him, pushing him to the floor. He looked up – amazed that he was still alive – to see Stiffkey standing over him, wielding a large shovel.

'I thought y-you'd left me!' stuttered Jake.

'I had,' said Stiffkey. 'But I came back.'

Pushing himself up from the ground, Jake saw the bonewulf's headless body lying on the depressing carpet and its severed head resting on the sofa, a look of surprise on its face.

Stiffkey stooped over to the coffee table and picked up a bunch of keys.

'You looking for these, boy?' He frowned as the skull toppled from the sofa and began rolling itself back towards its body. Stiffkey stopped its progress with his shovel.

Jake shuddered. 'What's happening? Why's it doing that? Isn't it dead?'

'It ain't dead. You can't kill something that weren't ever alive in the first place. A bonewulf ain't of the Earthly Plane – it don't have no physical form of its own, just takes what parts it can find. Be grateful you live on a farm and not near a graveyard.'

Jake shook his head. Believing in ghosts was one thing, but a bonewulf was another thing altogether. How had life suddenly gotten so strange?

He looked down at the mass of decaying animal parts.

And so . . . disgusting?!

Stiffkey scratched his chin.

'More bonewulf will come. Where there's one, there'll be its pack not far behind. And this one will reform soon. We need to leave.'

'Leave?' said Jake, panic starting to build again.

'Yes, immediately. Before their master, Mawkins, arrives.'

There was that name again: Mawkins.

'Who is Mawkins?' asked Jake.

'Not now, boy. We don't have time!'

'But what about my dad?'

'You ain't told him about the box, have you?' said Stiffkey sharply.

Jake shook his head.

'Then your dad is safe, as long as we ain't nearby. It's you Mawkins wants – and now it'll be me, too, since I've helped you and intervened in Embassy affairs. We're *both* condemned to the Eternal Void now. No doubt about that!'

'The eternal what?' asked Jake.

Stiffkey ignored his question and started pacing, wringing his hands with every step. He looked at Jake. 'We need help, boy,' he said, raising a long finger decisively. 'We need some help, make no mistake—' He stopped suddenly and clapped his hands. 'And there be one who might just be able to give it to us, but we'd need transport . . . and we need to take the box.'

Jake looked out of the back-door windows, his eyes settling on his dad's pride and joy – his campervan. Then he looked back at the bunch of keys in the ghost's hand.

'I just might have an idea,' he said, 'but Mum will kill me if we get caught.'

It was cold outside, and dark, and the fog was so thick Jake could barely even make out the licence plate – P368 ICL.

If you just looked at the letters, it spelt *PICL*.

Or Pickle, as Dad and Jake affectionately called her.

Jake felt a pang of guilt, but pushed it aside as he opened the door. He threw his rucksack on to the seat and climbed in, leaning over to unlock the passenger door for Stiffkey, who ignored the gesture and passed through the door the closed door.

Stiffkey hesitated. 'I ain't ever driven myself, and I'm no expert in automobiles, but I'm pretty sure a child shouldn't be driving one.'

'We've got no choice! I promise not to crash. Maybe.' Jake smiled nervously.

A snorting sound rang out from the darkness.

Stiffkey looked around. 'They be gathering, child,' he warned. 'We ain't got time for dawdling! They'll try to keep you trapped here till Mawkins arrives! Look!'

He pointed a long thin finger across the yard, where through the fog Jake could just make out several large shapes sprinting towards them. They were larger and bulkier than the bonewulf that had been in the house and were covering the ground at great speed.

Stiffkey leaped into the passenger seat, slamming the door behind him. A loud wet bang resounded as one of the bonewulf's heads made contact with the metal door. It backed off, growling. More bonewulf stepped forward. Four in total. They were starting to circle the van.

Jake turned the key, his hands shaking. Nothing. Once more. Still nothing. One of the bonewulf raised its snout in the air and screeched.

'It calls its master!' cried Stiffkey.

'Come on, come on . . .' pleaded Jake. He turned the key a final time and at last the engine coughed into life. He put one foot on the accelerator and eased off on the clutch, just as his dad had showed him.

Please don't stall.

Please don't stall.

Please . . .

The campervan jolted into life and lurched forward, careering through the scattered debris of the farmyard, out of the gate and on to the long lane that led towards the road.

'Look out!' Stiffkey shouted, eyes wide and staring straight ahead.

Jake flicked on the headlights. Other bonewulf had formed a pack at the end of the lane, blocking the exit on to the road.

Jake pulled hard on the steering wheel and turned sharply to the right, driving into the empty paddock. The van jolted and bounced through the long grass, until Jake saw a gap in the hedge, revealing the old wooden fence. Jake breathed in deeply and slammed his foot on the accelerator.

'Sorry, Dad!'

Jake winced as Pickle smashed through the fence. There was the noise of splitting wood, a sickening metal crunch and then, with a deft correction on the steering wheel, the van lurched on to the road.

Jake's heart was hammering in his ears.

'Well done, boy.' said Stiffkey. 'But you'd better keep that speed up, because that there –' he pointed out of his side window towards a small hill – 'that there is Mawkins.'

Jake looked at where Stiffkey was pointing. For a second he saw it through a gap in the hedge. Silhouetted in the moonlight, a tall hooded figure was wrapped in a thick mist, which seemed to form from beneath his tattered robes, snaking around his body and flowing down towards the farmhouse, like a river of fog. It might have been a trick of the moonlight, for surely he was too far away for Jake to see clearly, but the huge man – if a man it was – seemed to turn his head towards them, as if watching their departure. And then – as Jake accelerated the van round a corner – Mawkins vanished.

They'd been driving in silence a short while, when Jake glanced across at the sombre grey-faced ghost in his passenger seat. 'Are we safe from Mawkins now?'

Stiffkey frowned.

'All of us are born standing on the edge of a grave. Just a matter of time 'fore we slip. Mawkins ain't ever far away.'

Jake swallowed.

'Do you think your friend can really help us?'

'She ain't no friend of mine – not any more.' Stiffkey sighed. He turned to face Jake. 'And our troubles are far from over, boy. They're only just beginning.'

THIS IS REALLY HAPPENING

Jake could feel his heart racing.

The headlights of Pickle the campervan punctured the night, illuminating the thick hedgerows as they rushed into view before disappearing into the darkness behind. Jake had no idea how long he'd been driving for, but the events of the last few hours were all starting to feel rather unreal. He glanced across at the angry-looking ghost glowering at him from the passenger seat. If it wasn't for the indisputable fact that Jake felt more awake than he'd ever been, he might've believed he was dreaming – the bonewulf were most definitely the stuff of nightmares. And that figure on the hillside . . .

Still, at least he was alive. And this time he wasn't taking it for granted. Jake took a deep breath, composed himself . . . then remembered he was currently in a stolen campervan fleeing a pack of murderous animal corpses controlled by an all-powerful hooded death-bringer.

'I don't want to die!' He suddenly shrieked. 'It's not fair, I'm only twelve! How has this happened?!'

Perhaps staying calm was too much to ask just now.

Stiffkey sighed and gave Jake a reluctantly apologetic look. 'I suppose you deserve some sort of explanation.'

'Well, yes, that would be nice, if it's not too much trouble,' said Jake sarcastically.

'All right, boy, but I'd be reminding you to respect your elders, and they don't come much more elder than I,' said Stiffkey. He took a deep breath. 'The box you stole—'

'I did not steal it! You gave it to me—'

'Well, if you hadn't said your name was Goodmourning neither of us would be—'

'All right! It doesn't matter now. Just please tell me what on earth's going on?'

Stiffkey sighed and started again. 'The box you

have in your rucksack was a spectral container – its contents can be carried by ghosts or the living, on and off the Earthly Plane – and when you opened it, you invited a whole heap of trouble upon yourself. Because that particular box was *never* meant to be opened. Especially not by an unlicensed member of the living, who shouldn't know anything about it. So now the Embassy have sent Mawkins to find you, reclaim the box and banish you to the Eternal Void.' Stiffkey paused and drummed his long grey fingers on the dashboard. 'And now I've broken the Embassy rules by helping you, which means Mawkins will be coming for me too. Yup, we're in it together now, make no mistake.'

Jake glanced across at the grumpy old ghost. He had to admit, it was nice of him to come back and help him. If he hadn't, Jake would have been toast already.

'So who is Mawkins?'

'Mawkins is one of the Twelve Reapers, and the Embassy don't summon him often. They say he can track a man from one side of the earth to the next in the time it takes for the sun to rise and set, once he's got the scent, and now you've opened the box, he's got it all right. And each time you open it, he'll get the scent stronger and will be on you even faster, so you remember that next time you're feeling curious.'

Jake couldn't help but feel a bit sheepish at that. If only he'd never looked in the box, none of this would be happening . . . but it was too late for regrets.

Stiffkey stared straight ahead. 'He ain't like you or I. He don't talk. He don't smile. And he ain't ever been alive . . . So it means nothing to him to send a child to the Void . . .'

Jake shuddered – Mawkins did not sound like the sort of person you wanted chasing you across the countryside on a dark night. He shook his head in disbelief.

'This is really happening, isn't it?'

Stiffkey nodded slowly, and glanced across at him. 'That's the long and the short of it.'

Jake sighed. 'OK, so what is the Embassy of the Dead? What does it do?'

'The Embassy was created to police the divide

between the worlds of the living and the dead. It stands at one of the points where the Earthly Plane and the Afterworld are closest, and its rules and regulations are meant to protect both the living from any unauthorised uses of power against them by the dead, as well as protect the dead from any unwholesome spirits passing over into the Afterworld,' he explained. 'I worked for the Embassy for a long while, but then . . .'

Stiffkey turned towards the window a moment, as if lost in a memory, then turned back and brushed some dirt off his shoulder.

'Anyway, I decided to retire, but, as one of the most trusted members of the Embassy –' He straightened in his seat – 'they had one last request to ask of me – to hide and protect the box you now carry, until such a time as it were summoned back.' Stiffkey paused. 'Then a few days ago I was contacted and asked to take the box to a specific Earthly time and place and hand it over to an agent known as Goodmourning, after which I could return to my retirement. It was all top secret and it would have worked perfectly, if only you hadn't answered to "Goodmourning" and been able to see me, and then accepted the box like you were expecting it, and then gone and opened the thing and had a little look! Goodness knows what Goodmourning must have thought when he turned up and I didn't – not to mention what the Embassy must now think of me. A near perfect record, I had!' Stiffkey glared at Jake. 'I might be retired, but my instincts are still sharp, boy, and I knew something weren't quite right with you.' He pointed at Jake and narrowed his eyes. 'So I followed you home and waited outside, then followed you to the farm. I didn't know who you were, but I knew you weren't Goodmourning and I knew you had no idea what was in that box. And when I noticed my pocket watch was fast I realised it were all a big mistake. And now we're being hunted by Mawkins and both of us will get thrown into the Eternal Void sure as geese lay eggs.' Stiffkey rubbed his temple and breathed in deeply. 'It's a right old mess you've gotten us into, that's for sure.'

Jake grimaced. He was *pretty* sure it wasn't totally his fault but it didn't feel like the right time to mention it. If living through the 'Mum and Dad situation' had taught him anything, it was the power of a sudden subject change to diffuse an awkward confrontation.

'Those bonewulfs, huh? They were horrible! I can't believe we're not dead!'

'Speak for yourself, boy,' said Stiffkey, smiling to himself. 'I died a long while back.' He nodded at a signpost – a flash of white in the grey-green night – with a place name written on it: WORSTINGS. 'And that be our turn.'

Jake relaxed slightly as he signalled right. At least Stiffkey didn't seem quite as angry any more.

'And what will we find when we get to Worstings?' asked Jake, with a hopeful side glance at his ghostly companion.

Stiffkey's face darkened, the brief smile vanishing. 'We'll cross that bridge when we come to it.'

Jake looked across at him nervously. 'What do you mean?'

'Let's just say it were a misunderstanding. . . Another one. And the person involved ain't the sort to forgive and forget.' He looked out of the window. It was clear the conversation was over.

Jake shifted uncomfortably in his seat. He'd already driven further than he'd ever driven before and was getting tired. There might be motorways to contend with, and what if someone noticed a child driving a stolen van? Though, technically, he hadn't *really* stolen it. He'd just borrowed it. Knowing Dad, he probably wouldn't even notice it was gone.

Jake looked at Stiffkey. The ghost had picked up the phone and was turning it around in his long, thin fingers, examining it suspiciously.

'How come you can touch things?' said Jake. 'Shouldn't your hands just slip through stuff?'

Once again Stiffkey's mood seemed to brighten. Like Jake had touched upon a favourite subject.

'You be having a common misconception about us ghosts, so let me educate you some. Firstly, the word "ghost" is actually what they call a *blanket term*...' He stopped as Jake giggled. 'What's funny?'

'Well, you know . . . blankets. Like when you put a blanket on your head to pretend to be a ghost?' he explained.

Stiffkey frowned down at Jake, his whiskery grey eyebrows furrowing in disapproval. 'I find that quite offensive.'

'Sorry, Stiffkey,' said Jake. It was obvious that Stiffkey took offence quite easily. He'd have to tread carefully.

Thank goodness Sab's not here, he thought.

Stiffkey cleared his throat. 'As I was saying . . . "ghost" is a *blanket* term used to describe all spirits trapped on the Earthly Plane.' He scratched the transparent tip of his nose with the transparent tip of his finger. 'I be a *Spectre* – and a special sort of Spectre at that – but there's plenty more different types besides. The Wraiths, the Wights, the Poltergeists to name but a few. Anyway, the only thing we ghosts all have in common is that we were once in living bodies, but now the body is dead and gone, and somehow, for some reason or other, what you might call your *spirit* be staying here, on the Earthly Plane.'

Jake nodded. 'OK, that makes sense,' he said. Actually, he wasn't sure it did make sense, but then lots of the things he understood to be true he didn't really understand. Especially science stuff. Like, how did electricity work?

It had begun to rain so Jake reached across and switched on the indicators, then squirted the windscreen with more water, then finally found the windscreen wipers.

Stiffkey raised an eyebrow, but didn't comment, for which Jake was grateful. Sab would definitely have called him an idiot. Hanging out with more mature friends had its advantages.

Stiffkey continued. 'Aye, there are many different types of ghost. They can range from anything between invisible and visible or both, for example . . .' He faded slightly.

Jake blinked. 'Very impressive!'

'They can also have a physical presence.' Stiffkey rapped his knuckles against the dashboard. 'Or none.' He rapped his knuckles again and this time they passed through the wood. 'It's rare a ghost can do both and switch between them at will!

It's just us Spectres that can.' He smiled proudly. 'And, apparently, there ain't many Spectres that can do it as well as me. It's why I was recruited by the Embassy. I can carry things and I can drift through things. Both of which make you an excellent ghost to carry out Embassy business.' He frowned and looked out the window. 'Little good it's done me now, though . . .'

Jake nodded slowly. 'So what makes some ghosts different to others? I mean, what is it that gives you those superpowers?'

Stiffkey chuckled to himself, rather dryly. 'Superpowers, he says?'

He turned to look at Jake. 'You ask a *lot* of questions, boy, and to be honest a ghost tires of talking about the mechanics of haunting. I'll tell you this, though, and let it be an end to your bothering. There be some ghosts who have more energies than others, which means they have more ghostly "superpowers", as you say. And I've got a *lot* of energies. It's a curse and a blessing. It means I've got a solid form and can touch and feel, *and* it means I can be seen, or not, depending on what I choose.

But the problem with having lots of energies is it means I won't be moving on until it all runs out . . . The more energies, the longer the haunting.'

'Moving on where?' asked Jake.

Stiffkey gazed out of the window. 'To the Afterworld.'

'And is that what you want?'

Stiffkey nodded. 'That's what all ghosts want. When we're waiting to move on, we get the *longings*.' He sighed. 'It's like there's a thread from your heart all the way to the Afterworld, and all those that you loved that died and didn't get stuck, are tugging on it, trying to get you where you belong . . . with them.' He took his hat off, and brushed some fresh soil from it, before holding it in his lap. 'I just want to get on with the rest of my death and be dying happily ever after, so's to say.' Stiffkey gave a sad smile and fell silent for a few seconds, before continuing, 'But I'm stuck here on the Earthly Plane, on my own, till all my energies run out, and they're fading so slowly. I've got another two hundred years, or thereabouts. That's what the Embassy reckons.'

Jake couldn't imagine waiting for anything for

two hundred years. It was bad enough when his dad was five minutes late to pick him up on a Saturday. He felt bad for Stiffkey. 'Maybe the Embassy got it wrong? You might move on next week, who knows?'

Stiffkey almost smiled. 'That's wishful thinking, boy. The only way I'll move on faster is if I get Undone, but I'm a lost cause, and none of this will matter if Mawkins catches up with us and sends us to the Eternal Void.' Stiffkey shuddered.

'What do you mean, get *Undone*?' asked Jake. This time he was determined to get an answer.

The van swerved slightly and Jake quickly corrected the steering wheel.

Stiffkey shot him a disapproving look. 'That's something you'll find out when we get to Worstings, no doubt, so best you concentrate on getting us there for now, boy.' He took a deep breath and drew his hands down his face, making it sag even more than usual. 'Sure Bad Penny's going to have *plenty* to say on that subject.'

BAD PENNY

Jake looked across at the filthy terraced house on the other side of the street. They'd been driving all night and the sun was slowly coming up. In the breaking light he could see that once, long ago, the house had been painted white. Now it was a mottled green, smudged with the algae that had colonised the window frames and begun to spread across the walls.

Above the peeling doorframe an old CCTV camera had been ripped from the wall. Now it hung suspended from wires, looking like a robot spider in its web, waiting to drop down on anybody so foolish as to walk beneath it.

A few metres down the pavement a large hook-billed gull was pulling at a discarded piece of fried chicken leg, lifting it in its beak and shaking morsels of flesh from the bone. Another gull was perched on the broken guttering above the door. It looked at Jake with beady black eyes, tilting its head to one side quizzically.

Jake shuddered. 'Are you sure this is the place?'

The ghost nodded. 'Aye. I ain't going to forget this house in a hurry.' He grimaced. 'Though it's changed a bit since I were last here.'

Jake peered towards the far end of the street. The road dipped down and the town fell beneath the horizon, revealing a grey sea that merged with a similarly grey sky.

Jake took a deep breath and crossed the empty road, towards the house. He pushed open a creaking gate and was treading slowly up the short steps to the battered front door when he noticed Stiffkey fading from sight.

'Stiffkey!' hissed Jake. 'Come back! I thought we were in this together?'

'Probably best I stay disappeared till we're safely inside,' said Stiffkey's voice from somewhere behind him. 'And don't mention my name. At least, not till she's let you in.'

Jake looked nervously up at the door. The gull was still watching him.

Jake sighed and rang the doorbell. It made no sound. He pressed it again. Then he knocked on the door.

He stepped back, startled by the sound of a window sliding open above.

A small wild-haired elderly woman looked out. 'Go away! It's too early for callers.'

Jake rubbed the back of his head. 'Sorry. I know. We're –' he corrected himself – *'I'm* looking for someone called Penny?'

'Penny? Well, Penny doesn't live here,' she barked.

'Please, I need help . . .' Jake explained. 'I'm in trouble with the Embassy.'

The woman's eyes widened. 'Shush, you fool. Keep your voice down.' She looked up and down the road. 'Never know who's listening. Hang on. I'm coming down.' She disappeared from the window.

A minute later the front door opened with a sudden waft of stale air and damp walls, and she was standing before him, wrapped in a dirty pink dressing gown. 'It's been a while since I've been called *just* Penny.' She looked past him, up and down the street, then she beckoned Jake into a hallway piled high with boxes, and closed the door behind him. She looked him up and down, her narrow eyes twinkling slightly through her long, unkempt hair.

'You kids are a scruffy-looking lot these days, aren't you?' she said, huffing. 'What's your name?'

'It's Jake,' said Jake.

She smiled, revealing a startling set of perfect white teeth, then turned and disappeared into the squalid gloom. 'Funny sorts of names they give kids nowadays,' she muttered. 'Follow me, I'll make us some tea and you can tell me everything.'

Jake clambered over the boxes and followed her up some creaking stairs, leading to a dimly lit landing.

'Are you here, Stiffkey?' Jake whispered.

'Aye,' replied the ghost, surprisingly close to Jake's ear.

Jake jumped. 'Don't do that! I nearly died of shock!'

'Some of the best ghosts I know died of shock. And it isn't something to be glib about.'

'What was that? Did you say something?' asked Penny from the darkness.

'Nope! Just coming,' said Jake.

A cat was waiting at the top of the stairs. It was staring past Jake. Following its gaze, Jake could just about make out Stiffkey's form, like a trick of the light, or a wisp of almost invisible cloud that had by some fluke of nature arranged itself into the shape of a tall and spindly undertaker. 'Hello again, Pipkins,' came Stiffkey's voice, rather formally considering he was talking to a cat. 'Still alive, I see.' He didn't sound too pleased.

Pipkins hissed, turned in a circle and went back down the stairs.

'Cats.' Stiffkey tutted. 'Worse than children for seeing what they're not supposed to be seeing.'

Jake stepped through the open door into a room, empty except for a table piled high with newspapers and books, a tatty old armchair and a dresser covered in photo frames. Jake picked one up and blew off the dust. It was of a young, smartly dressed woman standing on a stage, looking as though she was smiling at someone next to her, but no one was there. A gleaming medal hung round her neck. Jake looked at the twinkling eyes – it was Bad Penny when she was younger, Jake knew it.

'Come along, dear,' Penny called from another room. Jake walked through a narrow archway that led to a small and messy kitchen.

Penny handed him a teapot. 'Put that on the table.' She picked up two teacups and followed him. 'Come and sit,' she said, motioning to a chair at the table as she sat in the one opposite. Jake did as he was told. He looked around nervously. He didn't know the first thing about her. For all he knew she could be a witch or something. 'Bad Penny' certainly didn't make her sound like a very nice person. He looked at her across the table. Until yesterday he hadn't believed in ghosts. Now he was wondering if this nice – if slightly grubby – woman was a witch. He felt guilty and forced the thought from his mind. *Of course she's not a witch.*

Bad Penny opened a tin of biscuits.

'Gingerbread?' she offered.

But then again . . .

Jake smiled politely. 'No, thanks.'

With a sudden movement, Bad Penny leaned across the table and grabbed his hand in hers, squeezing tightly, her bony, claw-like fingers digging into his flesh. She was staring hard into his eyes and it made him feel very uncomfortable. Like he was being soundlessly interrogated. Once Mum had asked what he'd spent his Christmas money on and then just looked at him until he stopped lying and admitted he'd bought some new trainers, but left them on the bus. That had been pretty bad, but this was worse. The longer Bad Penny stared, the more vulnerable Jake felt, as if she was piercing his soul.

Then, just as he was beginning to panic, she let go of his hand and broke into a smile, her white teeth flashing between her wrinkled lips and her eyes shining brightly.

'I can sense someone!' she squawked excitedly. 'I can sense someone through you. You've brought me a ghost!'

She clapped her hands together and stood up.

The smile suddenly dropped from her face. 'Stiffkey!'

She looked around the room crossly. 'Show yourself, Albert.'

Stiffkey faded into sight. He was standing in the archway. He took his hat off and held it awkwardly in front of him.

'Hello, Penelope. It's been a while.'

THE BOOK OF THE DEAD

Penny scowled. 'I thought I told you *never* to set foot in my house again, but here you are, poisoning the air like a sailor's fart.'

Stiffkey's long face took on a disapproving expression. 'Now, Penny . . . ain't no point in vulgarity. Don't help no one.'

She looked at Jake. 'What kind of trouble has this old fool got you into?'

Stiffkey ignored her and approached the table. 'Has the Embassy given you back your licence yet?' He sounded hopeful.

Penny cackled. 'Oh! Would that make you feel better, Albert? That even though you ruined *everything* – just when I was at the height of my career – at least I can still Undo ghosts in my *golden* years.' She glared at Stiffkey. 'I can't even make a cup of tea without needing a rest.' She sat down again, her voice softening. 'Take a look around, Albert. Does it look like I'm still earning an Undoer's wage? So there's your answer. They have not given my licence back.'

'I'm sorry, Penny,' said Stiffkey, sadly. 'Really I am. There's none more sorry than me. I wanted it more than anyone! I just don't know what's keeping me here in this wretched Earthly Plane with all you living folk and all your living ways.' He fiddled with the rim of his hat. 'I tried my best to be Undone.'

There was that word again: Undone, Undo, Undoer . . . Jake had had enough of listening and not understanding.

'Will somebody *please* tell me what Undoing is?' asked Jake firmly.

Bad Penny looked at Stiffkey, who shrugged his bony shoulders, dropping some dirt from his collar as he did. 'Go on, tell him. The boy knows far too much of what he shouldn't and he can't be in more trouble than he already is.' He looked down at Penny and the silence seemed to stretch between them until she sighed and turned her attention back to Jake.

'A spirit becomes trapped on the Earthly Plane due to an unresolved trauma during life or death.' She nodded to Stiffkey. 'You know why he's a ghost, don't you?'

'That's enough,' Stiffkey sputtered. 'Always digging for worms, you are. Like an old crow on a fresh grave!'

They were back to arguing, then. It reminded Jake of his parents before they'd split up.

Bad Penny cackled again. 'Such a dignified and serious man, is our Stiffkey. Not always, though – much to his misfortune.' She leaned towards Jake conspiratorially. 'The old fool slipped into a grave at a funeral he was undertaking. It was raining, you see. Snapped his neck.'

Stiffkey stood up and loomed over Penny. 'I forbid you to talk about it. It don't do, discussing the misfortune of others in such a way!'

Bad Penny whispered to Jake, loud enough for Stiffkey to hear, 'If you look close, you'll see the slight crick where the bones aren't set straight.'

Jake automatically looked at Stiffkey's neck then turned away again when he caught the thunderous look in the ghost's eyes.

Penny was enjoying herself now. She carried on. 'First thing he saw as a ghost was the horrified face of the vicar and the dead man's family peering down at his body lying on top of a broken coffin.' She breathed in through her nose and shook her head. 'Worst thing an undertaker can do is spoil a funeral. Isn't that right, Stiffkey?'

Stiffkey grunted, his furious face staring down at the floor.

Penny looked at him a moment, and then seemed to soften. She indicated for Stiffkey to sit at the table, which he did, begrudgingly. She poured out the tea, topping hers up from a small flask she retrieved from her dressing gown pocket.

'An *Undoer*,' started Penny, 'is someone who helps a ghost come to terms with their trauma – to understand why they're trapped on the Earthly Plane. They solve the mystery and that *Undoes* the ghost's problem. It cleanses their spirit and allows them to pass on to the Afterworld. Letting in resentful ghosts, or guilty ones, or furiously angry ones for that matter, would not make for a happy, peaceful Afterworld. Before they pass on they must deal with their issues, leave them at the gates so to speak, and then they're free to die happily ever after.'

Penny took a long swig of tea and then cupped her hands around the mug. 'And that's what I was. An Undoer – a member of the living licensed by the Embassy of the Dead to help ghosts pass on to the Afterworld. The living are the best at Undoing because other ghosts' energies can confuse things. It's much harder to Undo one ghost in the presence of another. I always like to do the final act of Undoing alone. Still, we living need help. Somebody who knows the business of the dead, and knows what it's like to be stuck. That's why every Undoer has a ghost assistant.'

'I was *not* your assistant!' grumbled Stiffkey.

Jake could feel the tension rising again, so he jumped in before it got out of hand. 'So an Undoer is like a brilliant detective? With an amazing ghost partner – like in the movies?'

'Yes, exactly,' said Penny, looking pleased with that description. 'I was an ace detective in my day. They didn't call me "Bad Penny" for nothing. Bad means "good" by the way,' she explained to Jake.

'That ain't why I call her Bad Penny,' Stiffkey muttered. 'She went sour a long time ago.' Penny didn't seem to hear, or at least pretended not to.

'Together we undid over one hundred ghosts. We were awarded the Order of the Dead Medal. Only four other Undoers and their *partners*,' she rolled her eyes, 'have ever managed that. We were set to break the record when . . .' She took a deep breath and glanced at Stiffkey, who finished her sentence.

'. . . When I asked to be Undone. I'd already been dead for over two hundred years and I was tired of the longings. We'd had a great run, hadn't we, Pen?' He smiled at her across the table. 'Receiving the medal with you by my side was one of the proudest moments of my career. But I just felt it was my time and I wanted to see . . .' He trailed off.

'Of course I agreed to help,' said Penny. 'Stiffkey was my . . . my best friend.' Penny smiled the saddest smile Jake had ever seen. 'Even though it would mean I'd have to carry on Undoing without him, find a new partner, I understood. I wanted him to be happy.'

Stiffkey and Penny held each other's gaze, before Penny carried on. 'It should've been easy. We were the greatest Undoers of our day, and we knew each other as well as any friends ever did. You see, ghosts never know for certain the reason for their hauntings, but with Stiffkey it was obvious. He'd ruined the funeral of another and he needed to make amends. We tried everything – tracing the descendants of the poor man whose coffin he'd smashed, helping out at funerals where the deceased couldn't afford a dignified send-off. We even reburied two people whose bodies had been mixed up at the undertakers . . .'

Bad Penny frowned and stared into her tea, as though remembering the past. 'But nothing worked and in the end we had to give up. It was never the same after that, not for either of us. We just couldn't *Undo* any more – not even the easiest cases. Eventually, the Embassy issued us with a deadline and when it passed they declared me unfit to be an Undoer and struck me off. Now I'm old and broke and still this sanctimonious toad wants to haunt me.' She looked at Stiffkey as she spoke, but the menace had gone out of her voice.

Stiffkey hung his head. 'I couldn't bear to see Penny hurting and know it was my fault, so I decided to retire and just wait out the longings away from other people and ghosts. Until now – now that we're asking for your help.'

Penny shrugged a little resentfully. 'Well, Albert, I just don't know. I don't see you for nearly twenty years – and now you want my help? Just because you've got some young innocent into trouble? I dread to think what you've done now.'

'It ain't my fault the child's sensitive,' snapped Stiffkey. 'And besides, you told me to never come back!'

And they were off again. Jake sighed, stood up and walked into the grimy kitchen. They didn't seem to notice him leave – they were too busy arguing. Jake heard the odd word being yelled – 'finger!', 'Goodmourning!', 'Mawkins!' – Stiffkey was clearly trying to explain what had happened, but there was so much shouting it was hard to follow. It was like being home with Mum and Dad again, and Jake had had about enough of that. He peered around the kitchen, looking for a distraction. His eyes wandered to a bookshelf filled with old, food-splattered cookbooks. Then one caught his attention, the only one with an unmarked spine. He reached up and took it from the shelf, turning it over in his hands. This was no cookbook. In silver writing, embossed across a faded green cover, he read the title: **THE BOOK OF THE DEAD**.

There was sudden silence and then Jake heard steps behind him. He turned round to find Stiffkey and Bad Penny watching him.

'See,' said Stiffkey, 'I told you he was sensitive. See how he found your book!' He sounded proud.

Bad Penny eyed Jake thoughtfully. 'So I see, so I see . . .' She took the book from him and put her arm round his shoulder. 'Come and sit down, Jake. I think it's time we talked.'

WHOSE FINGER IS IT ANYWAY?

'**Y**ou can have that book if you like,' said Penny, pouring out some more tea. 'Seems like you might need it.'

'Won't you miss it?' Jake asked.

'Oh, I know it all off by heart. Besides, I only talk to the dead through séances these days.'

Jake frowned. 'What are séances?'

'I help the living contact spirits who have passed on to the Afterworld. But sometimes I don't bother to contact them at all and just make it up instead. It's easier that way. It means the customers get to hear what they want to hear and you get bigger tips.'

She put on a calming voice. 'Auntie Julie's at peace. Her piles have cleared up and she's playing bingo in heaven.'

Pipkins the cat leaped silently on to the table

and began to lick around the edges of a tin of cat food that had been left open. Bad Penny gently tugged his ears, before looking up at Jake. 'But none of that helps you, Jake. Not now you've opened the Damned Thing . . .'

Jake blinked. *The Damned Thing?*

Stiffkey sighed and looked at Jake. 'She means the box and the finger inside it – the Damned Thing. I didn't want the job – I'd retired – but when the Embassy asked I couldn't say no. I had a duty to them, which I've carried out faithfully. A few days ago I was summoned and asked to pass the box to Goodmourning.'

'But why move it,' asked Penny, 'when it had been hidden safely with you for so long?'

'Well, I don't know for sure, but I heard that –' Stiffkey glanced around nervously, as if someone might be there, listening, before dropping his voice to a whisper – '*the body's been stolen . . .*'

Bad Penny put down her teacup and breathed in sharply. 'Oh dear, oh dear . . . this is bad news.'

'What body?' said Jake, looking between them anxiously, but neither of them replied. 'Is this related to the finger? And whose finger is it, anyway? Will *somebody please tell me what's going on?!'*

Stiffkey's face seemed to crumple in on itself. Jake had become used to Stiffkey's default facial expression. His skin hung from his cheekbones, like it had slipped slightly and no one had bothered to pull it back up. Deep lines were etched into his forehead – a legacy of a lifetime of worrying, plus two hundred more years of disapproving glances. Still, Jake had never seen him look more frowny than he did at that exact moment.

'As I told you earlier, there are twelve reapers in the Afterworld,' Stiffkey began. 'All as old as time itself. They ain't been people like you or I. They've never been alive – they're of the Afterworld. One of those reapers be Mawkins. Another –' he swallowed nervously – 'was Fenris.' He stared hard at Jake. 'Fenris were a wrong 'un. Not content with being one of the most powerful beings in the Afterworld, he wanted to tear down the barrier that has always existed between the Afterworld and the Earthy Plane, in order to use his Old Magic to gain more control over the living. But his plot was discovered and the Embassy of the Dead was founded to enforce what everyone knows is best for both living and dead – that their worlds be kept apart. A strict set of three rules was laid down to govern any movement or communication between those worlds – what contact the dead may have with those on the Earthly Plane; which souls may pass from the Earthly Plane on to the Afterworld; and, finally, outlawing the use of Old Magic, for its power was too easily manipulated. The rules were to be governed by the Embassy and enforced by the Twelve Reapers of the Afterworld . . . or rather, eleven, with Fenris to be thrown into the Eternal Void.'

Stiffkey leaned closer to Jake. 'But the Embassy underestimated the power and cunning of Fenris and he escaped to the Earthly Plane. There he managed to inhabit the body of a composer called Dasaev, who traded his eternal soul for the gift of Fenris's power. He became the greatest living composer, while Fenris just waited silently and patiently for him to die. For when he was to die –' Stiffkey took his hat off and looked upwards – 'well, it would be

Fenris that travelled to the Afterworld, not Dasaev, and this time he would be able to complete his plan.'

'So what happened?' asked Jake.

'Well,' said Penny, picking up the story, 'the Embassy caught wind of his plan, and waited until Dasaev was dying . . . then they cut off his finger,' she mimed bringing a cleaver down hard on to the table, 'and buried the rest of him.'

Jake's eyes opened wide. 'But *why?*'

She peered over the rim of her teacup. 'A spell was cast. Old Magic. To trap Fenris's spirit for ever, by splitting it between his body and his severed finger, with the finger possessing the essence, so to speak. If the two are ever reunited, his ghost will return to full strength and, make no mistake, dark times will fall upon the Earthly Plane. There are some powerful beings on the other side who would like nothing more than to be able to enter the Earthly Plane and wreak havoc. Old Magic would be back and the living would become mere playthings for the dead. But without a leader, without Fenris, their voices are silenced and the Embassy is able to keep things in check. So you see, it's imperative that the finger not fall into the wrong hands . . .'

'So let's destroy the finger!' said Jake excitedly. 'Why keep it in a box? Let's . . . let's burn it!'

'If only it were that simple. But you can't destroy a spirit,' explained Penny. 'If you destroyed the finger, you'd only set the spirit free. The Old Magic that binds it to the finger at least keeps the spirit in one place, controlled, and the lead lining on the box protects and strengthens that Old Magic, and keeps the scent of the Damned Thing in so it can't be tracked.'

'What *is* Old Magic?' asked Jake.

Stiffkey shook his head. 'It ain't magic like wands and wizards. It's the ways of the ghosts of old, ways that for centuries were handed down from generation to generation – until the rules were agreed. Some of the living are born with some of those ways.' He looked at Jake gravely. 'That's how come you're sensitive. But you'd do well to leave them alone.'

Jake blushed. He didn't feel like he had any special powers. Apart from being able to see Stiffkey. And, given his current situation, that seemed to have been a disadvantage.

Stiffkey shook some dirt from his cuffs and continued. 'And now the Embassy is facing a crisis again. The composer's body has been stolen, which means Fenris must have supporters working for the Embassy and the location of the finger may also be known. I was given the top secret mission to meet Goodmourning – their most trusted Undoer – so the finger could be protected in a new location.'

Bad Penny threw her hands up. 'But you gave it to a child instead!'

Stiffkey frowned. 'There's no need to keep reminding me! And now the Embassy will have sent Mawkins to track us down. They'll do anything to get the finger back – they might even think we're trying to help Fenris. That I'm a traitor!' Stiffkey's mind seemed to be whirring now, and he staggered back from the table as if in physical pain. 'But then, what do our lives matter if the safety of the Earthy Plane and the Afterworld be at stake?' He looked at Jake with wild eyes and said, 'I thought I could think up a way out of this mess, but we have to turn ourselves in, boy! It's the only thing left to do.'

Jake swallowed. 'And what will happen to me? Will I be killed?'

'Oh no, boy,' said Stiffkey, and Jake relaxed for a moment. 'We'll be sent to the Eternal Void. That be much worse!'

Jake's eyes widened in terror. Bad Penny placed one hand on Jake's arm, and the other on Stiffkey's, urging him to sit again. 'Calm down, Albert,' she said. 'You always were one for panicking.' She took a sip of the tea. 'If the Embassy has been betrayed from within, then we need to think carefully before returning the Damned Thing to any of their agents – even Goodmourning. What we need is a way to get Mawkins off your back – that will buy you some time at least. He'll be tracking you and even if you don't open the box again, he'll find you eventually, now he's got the scent . . .'

She placed her cup back on the saucer. 'You always were a good one, even if you are a self-righteous old fool. And you done right coming here, for there is someone I can ask to give you some advice . . .' She shook her head. 'But I haven't travelled for a while and I'm not sure if I can any more.'

Jake screwed his face up in confusion. 'I don't understand? Travel where? We can go in the campervan if that helps?'

Bad Penny gave a little laugh. 'Not that sort of travel, dear. I mean travel to the *in between*. The man who we can ask for help is an expert in all matters of the Afterworld. But I'll need to take Jake with me. My powers aren't what they used to be – I won't be able to travel for long. I can get you there, and I can get you back, and that's as good as I can do, but it will be worth it if you can speak with Mr Sixsmith.'

Stiffkey stood up again abruptly, pushing his chair back. 'No, I won't allow it. Not Mr Sixsmith. He's a Summoner! They be very dangerous.'

Penny looked up at Stiffkey. 'Don't worry, I'll make sure that Mr Sixsmith behaves.' She patted Stiffkey's hand comfortingly, and toasted him with her flask 'You can trust me. I'm an expert in handling spirits.'

Stiffkey shook his head. 'Well, it don't look like we've got much choice, boy.'

There was a buzzing in Jake's pocket and he

retrieved his phone. It was a message from Sab.

What time you getting here idiot?

He looked at the time and panicked – it was almost ten am. The bus would be stopping near his dad's soon, and he would be expected at school soon after.

Bad Penny and Stiffkey were looking at him, waiting for an answer.

'OK, fine,' he said, 'I just have to do one thing first.'

A NASTY CASE

'Hello?' said the voice at the end of the phone.

Jake paused. Then he coughed and tried to make his voice as deep as possible. 'Hello. This is Jake Green's dad speaking. I'm afraid Jake won't be coming on the school trip this week. He seems to have come down with a sudden case of . . . erm . . .'

Jake wished he'd gone through the conversation with the school secretary in his head before making the phone call.

He looked at Stiffkey for help.

The old ghost shrugged. 'Rheumatics? Used to plague me something chronic.'

Jake shook his head. He covered the mouthpiece. 'My mind's gone blank!' he hissed, looking at Bad Penny now.

'I get awful corns?' offered Bad Penny.

Jake winced and removed his hand from the phone.

And then it blurted out of him.

'Diarrhoea!' he said, inwardly groaning. It was the only illness he could think of. 'Jake has a severe case of diarrhoea.'

It wasn't perfect, but it was better than nothing. Which, he thought to himself, was more than you would normally say about a severe case of diarrhoea.

There was a pause and then, 'Diarrhoea? Jake Green, you say?'

Jake could picture the secretary's face. Her mouth all puckered up in disgust. Then her voice came back. 'OK, Mr Green. Thank you very much for calling. I'll make sure the teacher responsible gets your message. Goodbye.'

Jake breathed a sigh of relief. That was the not-so-small matter of not letting Mum or Dad find out that he wasn't on the school trip. Now he could concentrate on not getting sent to the Eternal Void. He had till Friday, when he was due home, to solve the problem, or else Mum would find out he was missing and she'd be after him, as well as Mawkins. To be honest, he wasn't sure which was scarier.

SUMMONERS

GHOST TYPE: Summoner

OCCURRENCE:

Summoners are rarely encountered and only a few have ever been successfully identified by the Embassy of the Dead.

DIAGNOSIS:

Most are misdiagnosed during the initial Embassy audit as Spectres (see p.110), their identifying powers usually becoming apparent only some years after death. In actuality, a Summoner is a type of Wight (see p.126) and is best identified by its predatory behaviour, rather than any physical difference from a Spectre.

CHARACTERISTICS:

Chiefly, their parasitic nature. Like most Wights, Summoners are malign spirits that inadvertently prolong their time on the Earthly Plane by sapping the spectral energy of the living (see Chapter 16: Illegal acts, Forbidden Substances & Spirit Addiction). While the Common, Shadow and Barrow Wight draw spectral energy from the spirits of the living through touch, the Summoner absorbs energy from free spirits already removed from their physical form (see Chapter 7: Near Death Experiences, and Chapter 8: Translocation.) Because a physical form is absent, the Summoner can draw these free spirits from great distances. With their typical lack of understanding, the living can believe that they have summoned the Summoner. In fact it is the other way round. The living spirit has simply made its presence known to the Summoner.

HANDLING ADVICE:

While it is not forbidden for a licensed member of the living to communicate with a Summoner, caution is urged if the body is left unoccupied, as the steady depletion of spirit energy caused by separation can lead to death.

Mr Sixsmith

Jake watched the flame of the candle dancing. Opposite him sat Bad Penny, the flickering light illuminating her softly wrinkled face in the otherwise blacked-out room. He looked around at Stiffkey. He stood nervously at the edge of the room, still shaking his head with disapproval.

'Keep looking at the flame,' Bad Penny said and, just as she had done earlier, she reached across the table and grabbed Jake's hands. She smiled at him and slowly closed her eyes, before starting a loud and tuneless humming.

She stopped suddenly and let go of Jake's hands.

'Goodness me, I forgot something!' She reached up to her mouth, took out her perfect white teeth and laid them on the table.

'They interfere with our signal,' she explained, wiping her hand on the tablecloth. 'He has to be able to pick us up or we'll just be floating uselessly above the table. Now close your eyes,' she said, taking his hands in hers and starting up her humming again. Jake took one last traumatised look at the false teeth, glistening with fresh saliva, and closed his eyes.

The humming was a strange sound, slowly

changing in note, first rising higher and higher, then swinging back to a low drone.

At first Jake felt a bit embarrassed. But after a while he couldn't help marvelling at Penny's ability to endlessly hum for ages without taking a breath. In the darkness, time seemed to pause. The imprint of the candle's flame formed a pinprick of white light on the inside of Jake's eyelids. First flickering and jumping like the candle, then slowly centring in his vision as a white circle – like daylight at the end of a long tunnel, growing nearer and nearer, and warmer and warmer, until Jake was bathed in a bright light. He realised his eyes were now open, and dazzled by the warm sunlight shining through his strangely translucent form.

Jake had left his body! Jake had left Worstings.

He looked around. He appeared to be sitting in some sort of waiting room. Through a large glass window he could see the skyscrapers of a city that seemed to stretch endlessly into the distance. Sitting beside him, eyes closed, was the transparent form of Bad Penny. The noise of the waiting room's air-conditioning mingled with her humming.

A voice spoke. It was a young female ghost, smartly dressed and with her hair pulled back tightly into a bun. She was sitting behind a large glass desk. On the wall above her head was a logo – a quill pen beneath the names WYATT & SIXSMITH.

'Hello . . .' She paused and consulted a screen in front of her. '*Bad Penny?*'

Jake nodded. 'Yes . . . er, well, no. This is Bad Penny.' He indicated the sleeping woman sat next to him. Her humming was suddenly punctuated with a loud snore. 'And I'm Jake. Should I wake her?'

The woman shook her head. 'There's no point. If she's not awake now, she'll be leaving soon.'

'Are you a ghost?' asked Jake.

The woman rolled her eyes and motioned to her translucent body. 'What do you think?'

Jake looked at Bad Penny. She was fading before his eyes and barely visible. Then, all of a sudden, she was gone, and Jake was alone.

The woman picked up a phone on her desk. 'Bad Penny has left a delivery.' She looked at Jake. 'A little boy.'

Normally Jake would have objected to the term

'little boy'. But at that moment he was on his own, in a strange place, with no idea how to get home and not even a body to call his own.

He'd never felt more like a lost little boy in his whole life.

Mr Sixsmith was sitting behind a desk, sweating profusely. He smiled as Jake entered. 'How wonderful . . . a new friend!'

He stood up and motioned to an office chair. 'Take a seat.'

Jake paused. Beneath Mr Sixsmith's shirt and jacket he was wearing nothing but boxer shorts.

Mr Sixsmith's eyes followed Jake's gaze. 'Ah! I forget . . . Don't be alarmed, just a side effect of dying on the toilet.'

He took a handkerchief from his jacket pocket and wiped his face. Jake noticed a neat hole in the middle of his forehead.

'The hole too, eh?'

Jake blushed. 'I'm sorry, I didn't mean to stare.'

Mr Sixsmith waved Jake's apology away, smiling. 'It's fine. I deserved it. Here's some advice for you. If you're going to steal money, take it from an orphanage, or an old lady, someone like that. Never embezzle from a mobster with anger management issues.' He sighed. 'Now to business . . . I'd heard there was a situation. I was hoping not to get involved. I hate dealing with Afterworld affairs. Luckily for you Bad Penny has put a lot of work our way over the years and I owe her a favour, or two. Shame she got fired. Take a seat!'

Jake sat down and started to explain. 'I—'

'Don't bother.' Mr Sixsmith waved his hand to hush him. 'I already know all about it – Wyatt and Sixsmith have eyes and ears everywhere. In fact, if that old curmudgeon Wyatt hadn't already passed to the Afterworld, he would be calling the Embassy right now and turning you in!' He leaned forward. 'I bet they'd offer a juicy reward . . .'

Jake shook his head. He didn't like the direction this conversation was going.

'Not for me. I'm not very important.'

Mr Sixsmith laughed. 'I was just kidding, Jake.

I won't tell the Embassy – client confidentiality and all that . . .' He smiled, but his expression was strange and unreadable. 'Right, to business. So you want to know how you can deactivate clause 7.3, huh?'

'Clause 7.3?' said Jake, frowning.

Clause 7.3 did not sound good.

Mr Sixsmith rolled his eyes. 'In layman's terms: you want to know how you can cancel the Death Order that has been automatically placed upon you by the Embassy for being an unlicensed member of the living who tampered with one of their boxes.'

Death Order sounded *even worse* than clause 7.3. Jake gulped.

'OK, I'll spell it out.' Mr Sixsmith sighed. 'You want to know how to call off Mawkins before he sends you to the Eternal Void.' He looked at Jake. 'Listen, kid, you haven't got much time, but your big problem's got an easy fix. Basically, you need to get yourself licensed by the Embassy of the Dead – that will make clause 7.3 invalid and Mawkins will be ordered to stand down. And the only way for the living to get a licence is to become an Undoer. And the only way to do that is to Undo a ghost – then you automatically get a licence. You follow?'

'I think so . . .' said Jake. He looked up at Mr Sixsmith, who still had a strange glint in his eye that wasn't altogether trustworthy. 'Why are you helping me?'

'It's the kind of guy I am.' Mr Sixsmith winked.

Jake wasn't a fan of winking. 'Stiffkey said you couldn't be trusted.'

'Stiffkey, huh?' Mr Sixsmith shrugged and looked out of the window. 'Can Stiffkey be trusted?'

Jake nodded. 'Yes. If you knew him you wouldn't ask.'

'Good. Cos the only hope for *you* is becoming an Undoer, but Stiffkey has other options. He can invoke clause 7.3's subsection c, so I hope for your sake he's one of the good ghosts, for there sure are a few that aren't.'

'What's subsection c?'

'Well, put simply: if he shops you and you go to the Void first, then he's not in trouble any more. You, though, will be straight into the Void.'

Jake blinked before saying, 'He's one of the good guys. I'm sure of it.'

Mr Sixsmith nodded. 'Lucky for you!'

He rested on the edge of his desk. 'You know what, kid? I like you. So here's some more advice – don't get hung up on this "good versus evil" garbage. In real life, and death, there's few that's simply one way or the other.' He took a translucent cigar from his pocket and looked at it wistfully. 'The finest Havana cigar. Two hundred bucks this cost. I was just settling down to smoke it when they got me. It can't ever be smoked now. I'm a ghost haunted by a ghost cigar. How's that for surreal?' He put the cigar back in his pocket. 'I miss them. You know, every one tastes slightly different. Everyone . . . Hmmm, yes. Funny how when you manage to lose one bad habit it seems to get replaced with another . . .'

He looked away from Jake. 'Trust no one in this world . . .' He seemed suddenly uneasy. Once more he patted his sweating face with a handkerchief. 'You should go.' He got up and came round the other side of the desk, reaching out a hand. 'Good luck, kid.'

Jake stood up too and shook his hand. It felt

damp and cold.

But something was wrong. It took a moment for Jake to realise. It was the way Mr Sixsmith was holding his hand, wrapping his fingers all the way around Jake's. And not letting go.

At first Jake tried to gently pull it free. Then he looked up at Mr Singer. His face had changed. Now his eyes were closed, and he was smiling blissfully.

Everyone tastes slightly different.

Jake tried to twist his hand free. He could feel his knees start to buckle. The energy was being sucked from him.

Jake could see that Mr Sixsmith was laughing joyously, but all he could hear was a high-pitched buzzing in his head, getting louder and louder. Jake fell to his knees, pleading, but no sound came out. Mr Sixsmith, the office, the city, were fading. The world was fading . . .

WHAT COULD BE SIMPLER?

A cupful of cold tea hit Jake in the face and he came to, gasping.

'Boy? Boy, can you hear me?' It was Stiffkey. Jake sat up and looked around, dazed. Stiffkey and Bad Penny were standing over him, Bad Penny with an empty bucket in her hands.

Jake realised with relief that he was back in the house and after patting himself down . . . yes, he was back in his body too.

'What happened?' gasped Jake. 'I think I was dying.'

'Aye, Jake, he was sucking the energies right from you! That's what them types do. Can't help themselves. Even though it prolongs their time here. It's sad when the thirst for energies outweighs the longings.' Stiffkey turned to glare at Bad Penny. 'It ain't right leaving a mere child alone with a Summoner!'

She looked at Jake. 'The boy's fine. . . You worry too much.' She rolled her eyes but Jake could see she was shaken. 'Do you have a solution to your problem?' asked Bad Penny.

Jake nodded. 'I need to Undo a ghost! Then I get an Undoer's licence, which invalidates clause 7.3.'

Bad Penny smiled smugly at Stiffkey. 'You see? Sixsmith may be a soul-sucking Summoner, but he knows his stuff!'

'Well, don't look at me, boy,' said Stiffkey. 'I'm like the proverbial Gordian knot. I can't be Undone.'

Bad Penny nodded. 'It's true. He's a lost cause. You'll need to find another ghost, and learn the basics of Undoing. Luckily for you, you've come to the right place! Follow me.'

Bad Penny led Jake and Stiffkey back through to the kitchen. She picked up **THE BOOK OF THE DEAD** and flicked through it until she found what she was looking for – a slip of loose paper pressed in between the pages. It was a list of names. About forty in total. All but two were crossed out.

'This was the last list the Embassy gave me to work on before they revoked my licence,' she explained to Jake. 'It's a list of trapped souls . . . ghosts who requested to be Undone. Me and Stiffkey had some fun solving some of these!'

She ran her finger down the list.

'I remember Ebony Bryce, of course. Died of old age, but couldn't pass to the Afterworld. She had no form, or visuals to her ghost – just a smell hanging around for near eternity. Until her cross-stitch was finished, that is.' Penny pointed to a cross-stitched picture on the wall. 'It took me a month, but the young couple that had bought her old house were so grateful.'

Penny's eyes ran down the list. 'Oh, and remember Bobby MacNamara, Stiffkey?'

'Aye,' said the ghost, almost smiling.

'He got trapped in the shifting mud when he was out digging worms for bait. Drowned when the tide came in. They buried him without his precious penknife. Well, we righted that, didn't we, and oh, the look of joy on his face as he passed on . . . Such is the life of an Undoer.' Bad Penny sighed, lost in the memory. 'We were quite a team, me and Stiffkey, weren't we, Albert?'

Stiffkey nodded solemnly. 'Aye, that we were,' he said.

Bad Penny looked at Jake over the top of her glasses and handed him the list. 'It was a good few years ago, but there's a chance that the last two ghosts are still out there, waiting to be Undone. Cora Sanderford, minor level Poltergeist, and Rose Buhari, a Spectre. It took us so long to Undo the ghost before Cora – the trouble we had with Finn O'Callahan!' She gave a little laugh. 'After him the Embassy moved us on to easier ghosts, but then . . . well, you know what happened. Anyway, I've still got their files somewhere . . .' She wandered off down the stairs and could be heard rummaging through boxes.

Jake looked at Stiffkey. 'It's worth a shot, isn't it?'

Stiffkey narrowed his eyes. 'Aye, but one day and one night only and then we have to get the finger back to the Embassy. Back to safety. Deal?'

The ghost spat on his hand and held it out.

Jake wasn't sure if ghost spit was real or not, but decided to do the same and took Stiffkey's cold hand. 'Deal.'

The spit was real. Jake tried to wipe his hand on his leg without Stiffkey noticing.

Penny walked back into the room with two files and dumped them in Jake's arms, along with THE BOOK OF THE DEAD.

'You probably don't read much, do you? Stuck inside on your playmachine all day, I expect.' She handed him the old book. 'It's out of date, mind,' she said, picking up Pipkins and scratching him behind the ears, then adding with a wink, 'but not as much as old Stiffkey is!'

Jake glanced down at the book and the files in his arms. 'Right, so . . .' he started, unsure of what it was he needed to ask.

'You'll be fine, dear,' said Bad Penny, reading his mind. 'You're sensitive, you've got the ways. All you need to do is talk to them, work out what's troubling them and why they're still here, and then you need to fix it: find something lost. Return something stolen, pass on a message. Soon as you do . . . *poof*! They're gone. What could be simpler?'

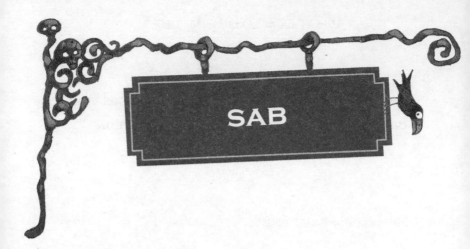

SAB

The text came through just as they were about to leave Bad Penny's.

Hey! Everyone says you have the runs?

In the last few hours Jake had almost forgotten about school, home and his friends. Being chased by a reaper will do that to you. He needed to reply – he couldn't risk Sab calling the landline and Mum answering. He would have to go along with the story and put up with the ridicule when he got back. If he ever got back.

Yeah, it's really gross. Have been to the toilet fifteen times today.

He probably didn't need that level of detail. He typed another message swiftly.

How's the trip?

Sab texted straight back.

Boring apart from when Tover fell in a bog.
That bit was funny!

Jake laughed out loud. The thought of that bully Ryan Tover getting soaking wet was pretty funny!

How's being ill? You got plenty of toilet paper?

Jake thought about Mawkins, the bonewulf and his recent brush with a Summoner . . .

You know . . . pretty boring actually.

THE SECOND MAN

Pipkins the cat slipped past the big man with the sloping forehead, who stood at the end of the street, smoking. The smell of the cigarette drifted in the cold air, but it was a different smell the cat was following. The scent of a second man. A man whose clean, freshly soaped smell trailed along the street and up the short stairs to Bad Penny's front door. Pipkins climbed through the catflap. Now the smell cut through the damp air of the flat, growing stronger as Pipkins padded up the stairs. The cat watched as a sharp-suited figure looked around the dirty room, smiling at the sight of Bad Penny, sleeping in her chair. She moaned and her head lolled to one side, her false teeth hanging unnaturally from her mouth.

The man grimaced. Behind him there was a

movement and he turned to see Pipkins leaping on to the table and settling down to nap.

There was a piece of paper on the table. He pushed the cat from its spot and began to read, ignoring Pipkins' angry glare. A smile spread across his face as he saw the two uncrossed names.

He turned to Bad Penny, reaching into his suit pocket to retrieve a pair of leather gloves.

It was for the best that there would be no fingerprints.

Bad Penny moaned again, turning in a fitful sleep.

The suited man slowly pulled on the gloves and took a step forward.

There was a knocking at the front door. The man paused, a metre from Bad Penny.

'We've come for the rent!' shouted a voice through the letterbox. More knocking. Louder this time. 'I know it's late but you can't pretend you're not in this time! Now open up and pay what's owed. This is your last warning before you'll be evicted!'

The man flexed his fist, making the leather creak. He turned from the sleeping figure of

Bad Penny, strolled to the kitchen and quietly let himself out the back door.

Maybe it wasn't her time yet.

Besides, he had more pressing matters in hand. The small matter of a boy.

A boy who had something he wanted.

THE BODELEAN SCHOOL FOR GIRLS

It was dark. Jake had driven from Bad Penny's along the windswept seafront. Soon the dirty arcades and boarded-up shops faded into row upon row of terraced houses that in turn gave out to endless fields, stretching over the rolling hills. From there they'd driven along the coast road, passing miles and miles of nothing until eventually, as the sun was setting, a large building appeared in the distance. As it grew closer, Stiffkey motioned for Jake to pull over outside a large pair of wrought-iron gates. Beyond the gates a gravel road wound through the grounds towards the grand house.

Jake peered into the evening gloom and read the sign that stretched above the high iron gates: THE BODELEAN SCHOOL FOR GIRLS.

The difference between Jake's scruffy school,

with its concrete yard and dilapidated bike shed, and this stately home surrounded by cultivated gardens was striking. A light flicked on – a single window among many – then flicked off again. It seemed that the school was asleep.

'Let's park the van out of sight,' said Stiffkey, indicating where he meant. A short distance along the road – on the opposite side to the school – a wooden gate opened on to a grassy field. Driving as slowly and quietly as he could, with the headlights off, Jake pulled into the field and brought the campervan to a halt, hidden behind the hedge.

'I would've liked to send my boy Sidney to a fine school like that,' said Stiffkey.

'To a girls' school?' said Jake, with a smile.

Stiffkey grunted and Jake immediately regretted the joke.

'I didn't know you had a son?' said Jake.

'Aye,' said Stiffkey. He changed the subject. 'Somewhere in that school is a ghost who needs Undoing. And you've got to find her, wherever she is.' He lowered his voice to a nervous whisper. 'Before Mawkins finds us.'

Jake nodded and shone his phone's torch at the file in his hand.

Cora Sanderford b.1977 – d1990
Type: Low-level Poltergeist.

'Low-level doesn't sound too bad,' said Jake.

'Read the rest, boy. You can't judge the state of a corpse by the flowers on its grave.'

Jake grimaced and then started to read.

'*Reports of a mysterious and sporadic knocking heard in the assembly hall of the Bodelean School for Girls, have been verified. It is my judgement that this is most likely the formerly unregistered spirit of Cora Sanderford (aged 13). No (0) visible presence. Little (0.02) physical form. No threat to the living. Minor Poltergeist. Priority: Low.'*

Then there was a scrawled signature.

'*Ezekiel Frost, Ghost Auditor, the Embassy of the Dead.*'

Jake raised his eyebrows.

'Well, boy,' said Stiffkey, 'if she's so low on spectral energies as to have no visible form, and only enough physical form to muster a little knock now and again, she might've passed to the Afterworld. But only one way to find out.' He took off his hat and brushed some dirt from the rim. 'But I hope I'm wrong, for both our sakes.'

Jake nodded and they both got out of the van and trudged their way over to the school. It had started to rain and the wrought-iron gates to the Bodelean School for Girls shone wet in the moonlight. Jake gave them a shove, but they were locked.

He wedged his foot on to a lower bar of the gate and pulled himself up, ready to climb.

'Well, I guess I'm going over and you're going through. See you on the other side,' he said, looking down at Stiffkey, then realising his error. 'The other side of the gate, I mean. Not as in the Afterworld. At least, not yet.' He gave a nervous smile.

Stiffkey shook his head. 'Dying is a serious business, boy. I should know.'

'Sorry,' said Jake. He really did need to start watching what he said.

Suddenly, the road was illuminated by the

headlights of an approaching car.

Jake froze. As the car started to turn in towards the school, he leaped back off the gate and hid behind a bush. A long dark car with blacked-out windows slowed to a stop at the foot of the drive. The front window slid down and a man's voice spoke quietly into the intercom. The gates opened and the car drove on. As the gates began to swing closed, Jake slipped through.

Jake crouched and looked towards the school. He heard a door slam. The car had parked and its lights were off. The driver must have gone inside. Jake stooped down and was about to run across the lawn towards the school when he noticed that Stiffkey wasn't following him.

'Come on.' He beckoned him over.

'I ain't going no further, Jake,' replied the ghost from the other side of the gates. 'I can't help you with an Undoing. It's harder Undoing a ghost when there's another one present, especially one like me. Bad Penny always preferred to Undo alone.'

'But ...' started Jake, a million questions running through his head. 'Can you at least look after the box while I'm in there?' he pleaded, beginning to rummage in his rucksack.

'I can't help with that either, boy,' said Stiffkey, shaking his head sadly. 'I wish I could. But those that break the rules must be the ones to fix them. It's the Embassy way. It's up to you to keep the box safe until we can return it.'

Jake sighed and reluctantly zipped up his rucksack. 'Fine. But how will I know when the ghost is Undone?'

Stiffkey started to fade. 'You'll know.'

Which wasn't the most helpful advice, in Jake's opinion.

But then Stiffkey reappeared. 'Oh, and be careful, boy – even the good ghosts can turn malevolent after being trapped on the Earthly Plane. And the ones that started bad . . . well, they don't get better with age.'

And with those words he disappeared.

Once again, Jake was alone.

POLTERGIESTS

GHOST TYPE: Poltergeist

OCCURRENCE:

Common.

DIAGNOSIS:

Poltergeists are usually formed as a result of mild trauma or minor disappointment at the moment of death. Examples of such include unfulfilled ambitions, imagined insults and the creeping realisation of insignificance.

CHARACTERISTICS:

A Poltergeist can be identified by the absence of any visible form and near-absence of any physical presence. They are capable of rudimentary communication with other spirits and the sensitive living through knocking, or through the displacement of small objects.

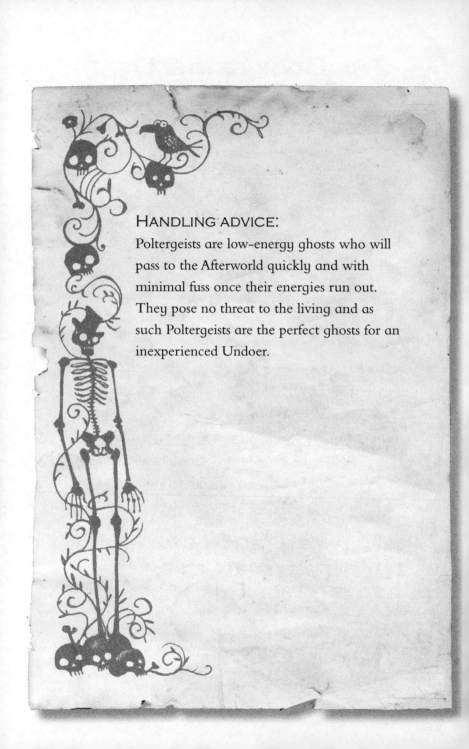

HANDLING ADVICE:

Poltergeists are low-energy ghosts who will pass to the Afterworld quickly and with minimal fuss once their energies run out. They pose no threat to the living and as such Poltergeists are the perfect ghosts for an inexperienced Undoer.

CORA SANDERFORD

Jake kept low as he ran across the gardens towards the school. The moon shone high in the sky, silhouetting the building, so it appeared as a giant black fortress, looming up from the ground.

The wind had picked up and Jake pulled his hoodie tight around his head, thankful for the howling that hid the sound of his feet as he crossed the gravel path leading to the front door. Not that he would be going in that way. He wasn't a total amateur, even if he'd never broken into a school before. Or into anywhere for that matter. It wasn't the sort of thing Mum and Dad would approve of and, to be honest, it wasn't something he'd ever imagined himself doing, either. Still, it wasn't every day you were threatened with the Eternal Void.

He imagined the response he'd get from his mum if he used that excuse – *'The grim reaper forced me to do it!'*

Unsurprisingly, breaking into a school turned out to be quite difficult. The main windows were, of course, all locked. Jake toyed with the idea of smashing a brick through one of them, but he was secretly relieved that there was nothing in sight he could use to do such an obviously illegal thing.

He skirted round the side wall towards the back of the building, once again keeping as low as possible. Eventually, the school wall turned the corner. And there it was: his chance. A small window left ajar, just big enough for him to climb through and just within reach. Besides, it wasn't breaking in if he didn't break anything, was it?

Cautiously looking around one last time, Jake jumped up, grabbed the bottom of the ledge and frantically scrabbled his feet up the wall, until he could force his head through the gap. A row of toilet cubicles looked back at him. There he stayed for a moment, catching his breath, his bum sticking out in the cold and his hood clinging to his head, looking like the least professional ninja ever. He wriggled forward until his weight started to pull him down into the room then, with a ripping noise, he fell head first into the basin, before tumbling to the floor.

He lay motionless for a few seconds, panting heavily. So what if it hadn't been the most graceful entrance. He had done it! He was inside the school, and there was no turning back.

He smiled at the thought of Sab's face if he knew that his friend Jake was a *dangerous criminal*. The naughtiest thing Sab had ever done was copying an essay from the internet. Mr Gillani, the English teacher, hadn't noticed. They had a theory that he just gave out random marks anyway.

Jake wondered what kind of student Cora Sanderford had been. The thought of her wiped the smile off his face. Maybe she'd passed to the Afterworld years ago and all this was a waste of time. Maybe she'd turned into some kind of super-evil Poltergeist, if they even existed. Maybe he wouldn't be able to work out why she was trapped here, at her old school, on the Earthly Plane.

Well, there was only one way to find out.

He stood up, dusted himself off and opened the door out of the toilets as quietly as he could, peeking it into the dimly lit corridor – it was empty. He crept out into the long hallway and tiptoed down it, painfully aware of the sound of his footfalls, until he came to a pair of heavy double doors. They were more like the doors you'd see in an old castle than a school – ancient thick beams of wood held together by black studded metal bands. He had to use his whole body weight to push one open.

That's when he noticed the chill.

From the darkness of the doorway he could see he was in a grand assembly hall. The room was cavernous – at least three storeys above his head. Huge wooden timbers spanned the vaulted ceiling and the moonlight shone through large arched windows, revealing that half of the room was full of rows of tables and benches, all laid for breakfast. He jumped as his knee knocked against a trolley, rattling the cutlery and a tray of condiments in little packets.

He picked up a sachet of ketchup and smiled

to himself. It was the same cheap, vinegary brand they had at his school. It was funny that even at this posh school, they couldn't stretch the budget to proper ketchup.

He stood for a second and listened. Silence. He walked into the centre of the room; he wasn't even sure what he was listening for.

Perhaps it should be the *quiet and sporadic knocking* he'd read about in the file.

Jake looked around. The heavy door he'd entered through was closed. Had he pushed it shut? He couldn't remember. He took a deep breath to calm his nerves. He remembered the words in the file . . .

No threat to the living.

That's when he heard the knock.

It was the kind of noise that you might have mistaken for the clanking of an old radiator or something. That's what a grown-up would've said, or someone who wasn't 'sensitive', perhaps. Maybe that's what *sensitive* meant. Just being open. Open to accepting that not everything had a logical or mundane explanation. Open to being curious. Open to questioning what a sound *really* was.

Then the knock sounded again – louder this time. Jake felt it was coming from the other side of the stage. He slowly walked across the floor towards what seemed to be the source of the sound: a glass-fronted cabinet next to the stage.

The cabinet contained trophies. They weren't like the ones in his school – tacky wooden shields, plastic cups, or badly moulded figures on fake marble plinths – these were *real* trophies. Probably real gold and silver, Jake thought. He cast his eyes along the cabinet's shelves.

He stopped. An inscription on a small silver trophy had caught his eye.

'The Cora Sanderford Memorial Award for Sporting Excellence,' he whispered.

Cora Sanderford! His Poltergeist!

Rain started spattering at the windows. It hadn't looked stormy outside, but it was coming down hard now.

Jake swallowed and looked round the room again.

'Hello?' he said quietly into the gloom. 'Cora? I'm here to help you move on.' He tried to sound confident but his voice came out all weak and reedy, shaking with nerves.

There was another knock – louder this time – and closer too, so that Jake nearly jumped out of his skin. He tried to breathe and stay calm.

No threat to the living.

'Cora? Is that you?' he tried again.

He looked back at the silver trophy. He noticed that of all the trophies in the cabinet this was the only one that wasn't straight. Jake pressed his hands against the glass and, finding it unlocked, slid the door open.

He reached in and picked up the trophy. It was small enough to fit in the palm of his hand. He flicked open the tiny lid, marvelling at its precise silver hinges.

At first the noise sounded like a breeze – a whispering sound that built, louder and louder still, rushing around his head. Until it was howling like a gale, forcing him to cover his ears.

'I want to help you!' Jake shouted. His heart was racing and his legs felt like they were on the point of collapse.

No threat to the living.

There was a crack to the side of his head. Not too hard, more like a slap, but enough to make him stagger to one side.

No threat to the living.

He spun round but there was nobody there. He felt a wetness drip down his forehead and instinctively touched it with his fingers.

No threat to the living.

He looked at his hand.

It was red.

Blood red.

That's when everything went black.

FREED

'Ohhhh, Precious is *finally* waking up.'

A girl's voice sounded from the darkness. It took a second for Jake to understand that his eyes were closed. He groaned and sat up. He could see the vaulted ceiling of the school assembly hall and the high arched windows. It was still night. He felt his head. The patch where it had been wet with blood was now dry and matted.

'I can't believe you fainted, Precious,' said the voice. 'I thought you'd died. You gave me a fright!'

Jake spun round. Behind him a girl sat on the edge of the stage examining her nails. She was wearing exactly the kind of school uniform that Jake would have expected someone at the Bodelean School for Girls to wear. White knee-high socks,

a grey skirt, a maroon blazer and a straw hat with a maroon ribbon. She had brown eyes and short, sandy-coloured hair.

'*Gave you a fright?*' said Jake.

'It was only ketchup, you know. A joke,' she said, rolling her eyes. 'I get awfully bored here.'

Jake blinked in confusion. The red on his fingers had congealed. He smelt his hand. It was vinegary, low-budget ketchup.

'Are you Cora?' he asked, although he already knew she was.

She sniffed. 'Yes, I am. Who wants to know?'

'Erm, I'm Jake. I've come to help you pass on to the Afterworld. To Undo you.'

The girl hopped off the stage on to the floor. As she did so, she reached her hand into the air and a hockey stick materialised there. She stood over Jake where he lay, leaning on her hockey stick as if it were a cane, and looked down at him dismissively.

'*You* are going to Undo *me*?'

'Um, yup that's right!' said Jake as confidently as he could. 'I'm an Undoer.'

'I can't believe you can even see me!' Her eyes

shone with excitement. 'You're the first person ever, I think.'

'Er, yup,' he replied. 'I'm a very sensitive person.'

Cora laughed. 'Awww, bless you. You are precious.'

'Not sensitive like *that*,' said Jake defensively, standing up and brushing himself down. 'As in, I have, you know –' he tried to remember what Stiffkey had said – '*ghostly ways.*'

He pulled a serious face, trying to look professional, which was quite hard considering the ketchup that was running down his face.

'I'm an *Undoer*,' Jake continued. 'Here to help you pass on to the Afterworld.'

'Huh.' Cora took a moment to ponder this before giving Jake a sly smile and saying, 'What if I don't want to "pass on"?'

He picked a scab of dried ketchup from his hair and said, 'Well, *all* ghosts want to go to the Afterworld, don't they? To stop the longings. That's what Stiffkey says.'

Cora raised an eyebrow. 'Who's Stiffkey?'

'Er, my ghost assistant,' said Jake. Well, he

was in a way. 'Stiffkey says longings are sort of strange feelings you get – like, a longing to be in the Afterworld.' He thought back to his conversation with Stiffkey. 'Like a string tied to your heart, or something. And someone's pulling it.'

Cora shrugged. 'It sounds dreadful. I've only met one other ghost before and he was dreadful too – didn't even bother to talk to me properly. Just listened to me knocking inside my trophy.'

'That must have been Ezekiel Frost, the auditor listed in your file!' said Jake. 'He thought you were a Poltergeist because they can only make noises. He didn't realise you were visible too.'

'But I'm not visible,' said Cora sadly. 'You're the first person who's ever seen me. I can only pop out for short spells when someone opens the lid, and no one has ever noticed me, even when I shout at them! And when I've been free for longer stretches, like in 2003 when a cleaner left the lid up and I had three days of freedom, the other girls couldn't see me and I could only wander thirty or so meters from my trophy.'

'That sounds pretty bad,' Jake sympathised.

'It is!' exclaimed Cora. 'When I'm in the trophy it's like I'm hibernating. Once I popped out and a whole year had gone by, but it had only felt like moments. It's awfully disorientating.' She leaned back against the stage and twirled her hockey stick around, and as she did so it seemed to glimmer. 'I entertain myself by scaring the other girls when I can – sometimes I can move the trophy from the inside and make it knock against the wall of the cabinet, but even pranks wear thin when you never get the credit.' She sighed, but then looked hopeful. 'Although, now you can see and hear me, and –' she smiled – 'did you say I have a file?'

'Yes,' said Jake. 'It says you're a low-priority ghost.'

She glared at him.

Jake looked at the trophy lying on the floor beside him. The lid was open. He went to pick it up. 'So if I—'

'No!' Cora put her stick between his hand and the trophy. 'Don't you dare close it! I'm not going back in there!'

'OK, don't worry,' said Jake. 'I won't touch it,

I promise.' Jake scratched his head. 'And anyway, if I Undo you, you'll never have to go in the trophy again. You'll be free to roam in the Afterworld. So it would be great if you could help me figure out why you're stuck here.'

Cora seemed to be thinking this over before she said, 'So, if you Undo me, I could leave the school. *Finally*.' She looked at Jake with wide eyes before walking over to the trophy cabinet.

'You know, I was so good at sport they named an award after me – soon to become my prison. I was here when they did the memorial assembly too. That was my first day as a ghost.'

She looked up at the vaulted ceiling. 'It's *so* boring being stuck here – it's killing me!' Cora rolled her eyes dramatically. 'Or at least it would be if I wasn't already dead.'

'How did you die?' asked Jake.

Cora inspected her nails.

'That's none of your business.'

'Sorry,' said Jake. He probably wouldn't want to tell a stranger how he died, either.

Cora climbed back on to the stage and stood

behind a lectern as though she were about to address an assembly of children.

'So cruel that one so talented should be taken in the prime of her life!' She looked down at Jake. 'That's what Mrs Fentiman said. Silly old bird. If they'd wanted to remember me properly they could have at least awarded me the Head Girl Cup. I was definitely going to get it that term, but it went to Agnes Petherton instead.' She paused for a second. 'It's not boasting when it's true.' She shrugged. 'Wendy Spithurst told me when she came to visit me in hospital. Spiteful if you ask me. The greedy cow ate all my grapes then told me they'd given the award to Agnes. Seems a bit mean to be bumped off the Head Girl spot just because you're on your deathbed.'

Jake looked up at Cora excitedly. 'Maybe you're trapped because you weren't made Head Girl! And if we add your name to the cup you'll be Undone . . . That's it! I know it is.'

She yawned. 'No.'

'What do you mean, no?' Jake frowned. 'You could at least try it.'

'Goodness, you are a dullard, Precious. Even if I did want you to Undo me that wouldn't work. And anyway, I don't want to be Undone. Because I know precisely *why* I'm a ghost.'

Jake looked at her. 'Why?'

'It's what I think about when I'm in that trophy and it's what I thought about when I was in that depressing hospital . . . Trouble for you is that it will take some time to solve.'

Jake groaned. 'Great. Another problem ghost!'

Cora ignored the interruption. 'I'm a rare combination, you see. I'm exceptionally lucky to be from a very privileged background indeed. Of course you've heard of my father, Lord Sanderford?'

'Nope,' said Jake.

She pulled a face. 'There are lots of super-privileged girls at Bodelean's. But I was more than that. I also had talent. Straight As, captain of the hockey team –' she gritted her teeth – 'future Head Girl!' She waved her stick dangerously close to Jake's head. 'There was so much I wanted to do. So many adventures . . . I was destined for the most sensational life . . .'

She sighed and looked out of the window into the sky. She folded her arms crossly. 'Well, this is my last chance. You'll have to take me with you and I'll be Undone when I finally feel like I've lived a thrilling life, or rather, death!'

'You don't want to come with me,' said Jake. 'It's very dangerous where I'm going.'

Cora's eyes gleamed with excitement. 'Oh, please take me!' she said. 'I'd die for a bit of danger . . .'

Jake felt his resolve weaken. He didn't know how it felt to be stuck in a trophy for years and Cora clearly wasn't ready to go to the Afterworld. Undoing didn't seem like something you could force on a ghost who wasn't receptive to the idea. He looked at the hopeful expression on Cora's face and knew he couldn't leave her stuck inside her trophy.

'OK,' he said. 'I guess you *could* come with us. Until you've done enough to be Undone. But I'll have to close the lid, so I can carry the trophy. You ready?'

Cora nodded. 'Only if you promise to open

it again as soon as we're outside. I haven't been outside for so long!'

'Done.' Jake flipped the lid back on the trophy, before placing it in his rucksack. He smiled to himself as he walked back round the stage and headed over to the big double doors. He'd never met anybody like Cora before – living or dead. It was just his luck that the first two ghosts he'd met were impossible to Undo. But at least he'd found two friends in them. And there was still one last name on the list . . . One last chance to stay out of the Eternal Void.

And then they would be free to get on with their lives.

Or in Stiffkey's and Cora's cases, free to get on with their deaths.

As Jake pushed at the heavy door, a hand whipped through the crack and grabbed him roughly by the ear, lifting him on to his toes.

'Well, well, well . . .' said a stern voice. 'What do we have here?'

MR RAYBURN

Jake glanced at the clock on the wall of the office and rubbed his sore ear.

11pm.

He could feel the extra weight of the trophy in his rucksack. No wonder they called stolen property 'hot'. It felt as if any moment it would melt its way through the fabric and clatter down on to the floor.

The headmistress paced around the small office. 'I should really call the police. Breaking and entering is a serious crime, young man.'

Jake thought better of arguing that he hadn't *actually* broken anything. He didn't imagine it would help his cause much.

The headmistress sat at her desk and glared at Jake over her spectacles. 'How old are you, Jonathon?'

Jonathon?

The headmistress's use of the wrong name confused him, but he decided to play along.

'Um, twelve.'

She shook her head in despair. 'What are they doing at Blethwick. I mean, *really*?' she muttered.

Blethwick? Now he was *totally* confused . . .

'How did you even get here at this time of night?' She pursed her lips. 'I always said Blethwick was a bad school for bad boys.'

There was a knocking on the door and the headmistress stood up. 'That'll be your school driver, Mr Rayburn. Your housemaster phoned us not long ago to warn us that one of his boarders might be dropping in, and Mr Rayburn arrived to collect you soon after.'

The black car, thought Jake.

The headmistress opened the door. In the doorway stood a huge brutish man with a sloping brow.

'Mr Rayburn.' She smiled. 'Your boy has arrived, as predicted. I'm sorry you've been caught up in this farrago.'

Jake watched as Mr Rayburn bowed his head politely. 'Oh no, Headmistress, it's us at Blethwick who should be apologising. And little Jonathan here, as well, of course.'

The brute smiled evilly at Jake, showing a set of cigarette-stained teeth. He didn't look much like a chauffeur, thought Jake.

'Young love, eh, Jonathan?' he said. 'Little midnight visit to your sweetheart?'

Jake's brain was whirring, panicking, trying to piece together what was happening and how he was going to get out of it. He had no idea who this man was, but he knew one thing – he did not like the way Mr Rayburn was looking at him.

'You can rest assured, Headmistress, he'll be properly disciplined once we're back at Blethwick,' said Rayburn.

'And his parents?' she asked.

'They'll be informed too.' He shook his head at Jake. 'Lord and Lady Alfriston will be very disappointed, I'm sure.'

The headmistress nodded. 'That will be punishment enough, I'm sure. Well, it's been an eventful night . . .' She stared at Jake. 'You're lucky to have such a kind and understanding housemaster. And a school driver who's prepared to give up his sleep for such a needless errand.'

Rayburn gripped Jake's arm tightly in his large, strong hand and led him from the room.

'I'll see you both out,' said the headmistress, beckoning them down the corridor.

'Oh, that's quite all right,' said Mr Rayburn. 'We can see ourselves out. We've been enough trouble to you as it is.'

Jake was thinking fast, but beginning to panic. He had no idea who this man was. Perhaps he should tell the headmistress it was all a lie. But she'd never believe him. He had to think fast . . .

'Can I use the toilet first?' he blurted out.

Rayburn scowled. 'NO,' he almost shouted, then, gaining control of his voice again, added, 'We need to get moving.'

Jake looked up pleadingly at the headmistress. 'Please?'

The headmistress rolled her eyes. 'For goodness' sake. But hurry. I – and I'm sure Mr Rayburn too –

would like to get back to our respective beds as soon as possible. You can see yourselves out,' she said, giving Jake one last dissaproving look.

Mr Rayburn grudgingly let go of Jake's arm, and pushed him towards the toilet door.

To Jake's relief the small window was still open. He reached up, grabbed the sill and desperately pulled himself upwards towards freedom. He was almost through when he felt hands grabbing him roughly. Huge powerful hands.

'Don't even try it!'

It was Rayburn.

Jake struggled in his grasp but there was nothing he could do. The man was too strong. He stopped fighting and felt himself pulled back down to the ground.

'You're coming with me,' breathed Mr Rayburn, 'and you better have the box with you or you won't be alive for very long.'

CHILD LOCK

It was still dark outside, but the rain had stopped. Jake could see the parked black car that had passed them at the gates. Rayburn dropped Jake on to the floor and pressed a button on his keys. The lights flickered and the locks popped open.

Jake tensed. He looked around for somewhere to run. Every instinct in his body, every feeling, every bone was screaming out for him to run. Too late. He felt Rayburn's meaty hand gripping his hood.

'That would be a mistake. We're going to take good care of you, don't worry. As long as you show the boss where you've hidden his package . . . Don't worry, he isn't far away.' The big man scowled. 'Likes me to do his dirty work.' He wrapped Jake's hood around his fist and banged him roughly against the car.

Jake sagged to his knees on the gravel, and the man picked him up and effortlessly threw him on to the back seat. Jake immediately tried the opposite door but it was locked. He was trapped.

Seconds later the man was in the driving seat. The engine softly purred into life.

Jake watched from the window as the car crunched its way slowly along the long gravel drive. Somewhere out there was Stiffkey. Waiting for him. Counting on him.

He unzipped his rucksack. The box was in there. Still safe. And Cora's trophy too. He flipped open the lid, waiting for her to appear.

Nothing.

He peered inside the trophy. It was empty.

'Looking for me, Precious?' came a voice from the front seat. He glanced up to see Cora smiling at him.

'How did you get there?' he blurted out.

'What's that?' barked Rayburn. 'You just keep your mouth shut.'

Rayburn couldn't see Cora! Maybe he wasn't sensitive to the presence of ghosts.

Cora held up her hand and her hockey stick materialised in it. 'Want me to bash him?' She waved the stick threateningly.

Jake shook his head and mouthed the word *child lock.*

Cora looked puzzled. 'What?'

He pointed to the dashboard. *Unlock the doors*, he mimed.

'This one?' asked Cora, flicking the hazard lights on. Rayburn grunted and turned them off.

Cora tried another button. The radio came on. Then she tried the windscreen wipers, then the indicators. Each time Rayburn turned them back off. He was getting increasingly annoyed.

She laughed and pressed them all again. And new ones, loads of buttons all at once.

A woman's voice sounded from the satnav box on the windscreen . . .

'Resetting language to German. *Guten Tag.*'

'What the blazes?'

Rayburn leaned over and pulled the box from its suction cups. He shook it, then the car hit another speed bump and swerved to the left.

He dropped the satnav and braked suddenly as the car mounted the grass, but not quickly enough to avoid shunting into a statue of a former headmistress, causing Jake to slide off the seat on to the floor.

The car door opened. Cora was standing there, saluting. 'It's quicker just opening it from the outside.'

And just like that Jake was free and sprinting across the wet lawn, shoving the trophy back into his hoodie pocket as he ran, propelled by the elation of escape, running like he'd never run before. Behind him he heard the car door slam. He glanced back and could see the bulky form of Rayburn loping after him. He scanned around for Cora. She was nowhere to be seen. She had to be back inside the trophy. He must've closed the lid when he put it into his pocket. There was no time to check. Rayburn was gaining on him.

He sprinted for a copse of trees. It was still dark and they might provide some cover. He reached the trees but there was nowhere to hide, just the brick wall, topped with iron railings that enclosed the school grounds. Jake jumped and grabbed at the bottom of the railing, his trainers desperately trying to find traction on the bricks, but there was no grip. He needed to find another way out. Jake jumped down and heard a thud on the ground next to him. His pocket was empty.

'Cora!'

He searched for the trophy in the dark amongst the wet grass and dead leaves.

Rayburn's voice cut through the cold night air. 'Got you, you little . . .'

Jake felt himself lifted from the ground and then thrown on to the rough track. He lay winded, gasping for air. Looming over him, the chauffeur was holding a small wooden cudgel. He raised it above his head. Jake covered his face.

'Please, don't!' he said, shutting his eyes and waiting for the final blow.

It didn't come.

He opened his eyes. Rayburn was lying motionless on his back.

A familiar voice rang out. '*Please,*' it said mockingly. 'Please don't.'

Jake pulled himself to his knees, still trying to catch his breath, and leaned over Rayburn's body. He was breathing, but a painful looking hockey stick-shaped welt was beginning to form on his forehead.

'We'd better get moving, Precious,' said Cora, effortlessly climbing the wall, as she found seemingly invisible foot-holes and hand-grabs. She swung herself over the railing and lowered her hockey stick for Jake to grab on to. 'This thug's going to wake up soon and you've quite a lot of explaining to do.'

CORA SANDERFORD IS NO POLTERGEIST

Jake breathlessly flung open the campervan door.

'Heavens above, boy, if my heart hadn't already stopped all those years ago . . . What's the matter?'

'No time!' Jake turned the key in the ignition. Once, twice, then finally the third time it spluttered into life.

Jake turned on to the road and drove away from the Bodelean School for Girls as fast as he could. He didn't even know where he was driving yet – he just knew he had to get far away from the school before Rayburn woke up.

'Well? What of the Poltergeist?' said Stiffkey. 'Is she Undone?'

Jake shook his head. 'Cora Sanderford is no Poltergeist!'

'And I'm certainly not Undone!' added Cora from the back seat.

For the second time in as many minutes Stiffkey leaped in his seat and clutched at his heart. He looked at Jake crossly.

'What are you thinking of, boy? Ain't we in enough trouble already without a young lady tagging along with us? Despite where your Ma and Pa may be thinking you are, this ain't no school outing to the seaside!'

Cora looked the old ghost up and down. 'What have you come dressed as?'

'That's no way to speak to your elders!' scolded Stiffkey. He looked out of the window. 'Ain't I got enough problems with one child to look after?'

Jake banged the steering wheel. 'If you'll both stop talking for a minute and let me explain . . .'

Deciding they were safe for now, Jake pulled over and turned the engine off. He took a deep breath and then began to tell Stiffkey, as quickly as possible, what had happened. Which, as it turned out, was not very quickly, especially considering Cora was interrupting him every five seconds.

'You should have seen me wallop him with my hockey stick! Knocked him out cold!' she bragged.

'All right, all right,' said Stiffkey. 'I get the idea.' He held his chin thoughtfully. 'So most likely that man and his boss be those that stole the body, and they know we have the finger, which means we now be being chased by both Mawkins *and* them.' Stiffkey rubbed his hands down his face, looking more tired than ever.

'Well, looks like we'd better be finding our final ghost to Undo,' said Stiffkey. 'But if we have no luck there, boy, we'll have to be heading to the Embassy to give ourselves and this finger up.'

Jake took a deep breath, the reality of their predicament settling heavy on his shoulders. He leafed through Bad Penny's paperwork, looking for the last ghost's file.

'Who's Mawkins?' asked Cora, leaning forward from the back seat. 'And where's the finger? Can I see it? Is that what's in the box that man wanted? Crikey, this really is an adventure! I had no idea you had it in you, Precious . . .'

Stiffkey eyed Cora suspiciously. 'You ask a lot

of questions . . . You ain't no low-level poltergeist at all, are you?' He tilted his top hat slightly and scratched his wrinkly forehead. 'I be wondering how the Embassy got you so wrong . . . A ghost with only a slight physical form, it says in your file, capable only of knocking . . .' He raised an eyebrow. 'Well, you knocked that driver out by all accounts.' A smile crept across his face and Cora burst into giggles too.

'No, you ain't no Poltergeist, girl. . .' He paused for dramatic effect. 'You be a Possessor!' Stiffkey nodded to the trophy. 'And that there trophy's what you possess.'

'Why are you so obsessed with working out what kind of ghost I am?' asked Cora, folding her arms. 'Maybe I'm unique. Maybe I'm a new, special kind of ghost. What is it with people always trying to put others into boxes?'

Stiffkey looked hurt. 'Speaking as an undertaker, I can categorically state that there ain't nothing wrong with putting people in boxes, girl.'

Cora burst into giggles again at that, and Jake noticed that even Stiffkey couldn't help but smile.

'So, being a Possessor,' said Cora, 'is why I get trapped in that trophy every time someone closes the lid?'

'I'm afraid so,' said Stiffkey.

'Well, how do I stop it?'

'Ain't nothing you can do, girl,' said Stiffkey gently. 'It's just the hand death dealt. And now you've also broken one of the Embassy rules: the dead shall have no contact with the unlicensed living.' He looked around nervously. 'You be in the same boat as us now, girl, and sadly it ain't the one that takes you safely across the river Styx.'

'Is that where Rose Buhari lives?' asked Jake, still searching for her address in the file.

Cora looked superior. 'It's Greek mythology, Precious – the river you have to cross to get to the Afterworld . . . So what kind of metaphorical boat are you two in, anyway? You still haven't answered any of my questions, which is very rude.'

'Ah ha!' said Jake, at last finding what he was looking for. 'Tell you what, if you can help me get to here –' he passed back the piece of paper that showed Rose's address – 'we'll explain everything along the way. We've got a ghost to Undo!'

7.05pm

'Hi, Jake. It's Mum. How's it going? You didn't call. Hope you're having fun.'

7.10pm

'It's Mum. Call me, please.'

7.15pm

'Hi, Jake. It's Mum again. Where are you? Why didn't you ring? You said you'd call at seven every night. Call tomorrow! Don't think I won't call you . . . or your teacher! Hope you're having fun and being good. Love you. Kiss kiss.'

9.00am

'Hey, it's me, Dad. Just phoning to say hi. Oh,

and can you phone Mum? You know what's she's like. Speak soon, lots of love.'

Jake was in a queue in the garage – having reluctantly just pumped £19.98 worth of petrol into the campervan. Only 2p left of the money he had been given to spend on the school trip and a feeling of immense unfairness was currently coursing through his veins.

He didn't have time to call Mum and Dad back. Besides, he didn't want to get dragged into a deeper web of lies, lying not really being one of his strengths, although he'd definitely improved at it over the last two days. He sent them both a quick message.

All good, Mum. Will phone tonight, promise.

OK Dad. Will do.

Jake opened his message from Sab.

Idiot.

He replied.

Idiot.

Sab started typing back. Maybe there was time for a quick chat? He sort of missed Sab and wished he could tell him what was happening.

Sab: What's really wrong with you? It's rubbish here and cold. Bought you a postcard with a picture of a rock on it. Geology is boring but better than the runs!!!

Jake: Haha. I'm in bed. Still ill.

Sab: No you're not.

Jake: How did you know that???

Sab: Sedimentary my dear Watson. Your mummy wouldn't let you use your phone when you're ill in bed. I told you I'm an igneous.

Jake: ?

Sab. Igneous – it's a type of rock

Jake: And?

Sab: I'm a genius/igneous, idiot.

Jake: That joke doesn't work.

Sab: Not for a idiot, anyway.

Jake: Got to go! Catch you later.

Sab: Fine. But I'm coming round on Sunday and I want the truth!

Maybe Sab wasn't as stupid as he looked? Or, hopefully, he was just joking? Either way, Jake couldn't worry about that now.

'That'll be twenty pounds, young man,' said a voice from behind the counter.

Jake looked up and handed over the cash. It really was painful to part with it.

'Thank you,' said the man. 'Good to see a young man helping his dad out.' He nodded to the forecourt, where the shape of a tall man wearing a wax jacket and a flat cap could be seen on the driver's side of the campervan.

Stiffkey had not been happy about being a mannequin for Dad's old farm clothes, but needs must.

Jake climbed back into the campervan just as a lorry pulled up beside it, hiding it from the cashier's sight. Finally, some good luck! Stiffkey scuttled into the back seat, still grumbling, as Jake started the engine. They just needed this lucky streak to continue when they found Rose . . .

THE WHITE HARE

Mawkins knelt on the turf. The wet lawn sparkled in the moonlight, but where the child had stepped, no raindrops clung to the grass. The steps led across the lawn to the brick wall that surrounded the looming building. He frowned at the sight of the unconscious man, whose lumbering purpose in this malevolence was unknown. Once, long ago, there was a time when Mawkins would have been able to reap his soul to be on the safe side. But times had changed. Now he needed the authority of the Embassy. It seemed strange that ghosts should control the whims of a reaper who had existed since the beginning of time. But it was just the way things were now. The better way for all. Just a shame it wasn't as much fun.

He thought of the boy child. Many had tried

running from the reaper – living and dead – but none had escaped his power for long. He lifted his head and took another sniff, filtering out the scent of a million other creatures, until he found it again: The unmistakable smell of the Damned Thing – muted by the smell of its spectral container, but still perfuming the air with its deathly fragrance. It was on the move. He took a step forward. And another. And with each long stride he passed into the ground, merging seamlessly with the soil until he had become one with the dirt.

Rayburn groaned and rubbed his head. A large bump had risen on his forehead. He pushed himself from the wet ground and staggered back to his dented car. The boy would pay for this.

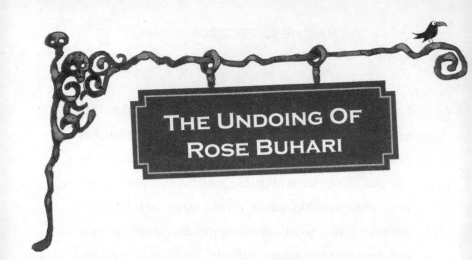

THE UNDOING OF ROSE BUHARI

Jake stopped. With one foot on the ground and the other lodged into the thick vine that grew up the ramshackle cottage. He looked over his shoulder. The fox had followed him across the front garden and now it paused some twenty metres away, its head cocked to one side in a way that seemed to be saying: I know you are up to no good.

Up to no good? thought Jake. *What do you know? My life depends on Undoing Rose Buhari.*

Does that give you the right to break into someone's house?

Jake shook his head and turned back to the house. He had to stop having imaginary conversations with a fox and focus on the task at hand.

Just before arriving at Rose's house Jake had

had to have a power nap, as Mum called them. He hadn't slept properly since Sunday night – it was now Wednesday! – and he couldn't keep his eyes open any longer. His head nodded, like it always did in double maths, and Jake reluctantly pulled over. Stiffkey had tucked the waxed jacket round Jake and told him he'd stand guard for a couple of hours and then wake him.

It had felt like only minutes later when Stiffkey gently shook Jake, who groaned and faced the other way. Cora used an altogether different tactic, whipping the jacket off him and shouting right in his ear, 'Wakey-wakey, lazybones!'

Jake grudgingly opened one eye and then the other, as the memories of the last few days came flooding back.

They drove the last few miles in silence. A serious air had grown between them. This was it. His and Stiffkey's last chance to save themselves. It had to work this time. It just had to.

Jake parked outside Rose's house. He slung his rucksack on and stepped outside into the bright afternoon light.

'Good luck, boy,' said Stiffkey, patting him on the shoulder.

'Yeah, break a leg,' said Cora. 'Or an arm.' She smiled in a way that could maybe be described as friendly.

Jake waved at his friends before walking purposefully up the garden path. He remembered the notes from Rose's file.

Rose Buhari b.1961 – d.1991
Type: Spectre.

Just a nice Spectre, like Stiffkey. A friendly ghost . . . What could go wrong?

Jake had looked all around the house for a way in, pushing through gaps in the thick hedgerow, wading through knee-high nettles. But the boarded-up building, all overgrown with weeds and covered in thick ivy, looked impenetrable from the ground. Then, looking up, he had noticed a small, broken window on the first floor as it winked in the late afternoon sun. Why couldn't he just find an open door for once?!

Apart from a slight wind rustling through the trees, everything was silent. He paused as he heard a sound. Did it come from inside the house? It could've been anything. A footstep, perhaps, or maybe just the creaking of the old house as it shifted slightly in the wind?

Jake reached out and tugged the ivy. It seemed fairly secure at the bottom at least. He reached up to one of the larger branches and began to climb.

He made slow progress and the leaves scratched against his face. Eventually, though, his hands felt the wooden ledge. Pulling himself level with the window, he poked a hand carefully through the broken pane and unlocked the catch. Then he jammed his fingers around the edge of the window and gave the frame a sharp tug. It swung open and for a split second he was lost, fumbling for a handhold, then his fingers caught the wooden rim again, the sensation of a splinter burying into his palm accompanied by a huge sense of relief. He gritted his teeth as little by little he dragged himself through the open window before collapsing in a pile on to the carpet, sending up a cloud of dust.

He was in a bedroom.

At first it seemed that nothing had been changed or moved since Rose Buhari's death. An empty cup stood on a bedside table. A dressing gown hung from the door. Everything was covered in a thick coating of dust. But something *had* changed. All the drawers in her bedside cabinet were open. A wardrobe door had been left ajar. Someone had been here since her death. Someone searching for something.

A cobwebbed photo frame stood on the dressing table. He picked it up. A lady around his mum's age. He wondered if this was Rose Buhari? She looked younger than he had expected.

He sighed as he felt a weird rush of sadness pass over him. Almost like he was about to cry. He swallowed.

Pull yourself together.

Jake pushed the drawers shut. It felt weird, them being open, revealing their contents to the world. Rose deserved more respect. He wondered why the house hadn't been cleared. She might not have had any family. He felt a wave of unexpected sadness. If Mawkins did drag him to the Eternal Void then at least he could count on Mum, and probably even Dad, to sort his things out and not leave his underwear drawer open for complete strangers to see.

He reminded himself that at least *he* was here to help Rose. She would want to move on to the Afterworld – she'd have the *longings*. In a way it was like being an undertaker, like Stiffkey. But instead of helping the relatives come to terms with the death of a loved one, you're helping the loved one come to terms with their own death.

As he went to close the top drawer, he noticed an old-fashioned personal CD player. He picked it up, blew off the dust and turned it round in his hands. He thought of his dad and his record player, how he always wanted Jake to listen to the songs he loved. Curiosity got the better of him. Jake pressed the open button and the lid popped up, presenting him with the edge of a shiny disc.

Beginner's Spanish.

Maybe Rose was going to move to Spain, but didn't get the chance? Or maybe she was just about to go on holiday? But then again, maybe she was just learning Spanish for the fun of it . . . Although, thinking back to the one term he had learned Spanish in school, he couldn't imagine anybody finding it that fun.

'*El gato negro*,' Jake muttered to himself. Names and colours of animals was basically all the Spanish he had. Useful if he ever needed to buy a black cat from a Spanish pet shop.

Carefully he closed the lid and placed the CD player back in the drawer, gently pushing it shut.

The trip to Spain, the loneliness . . . All things that might be to do with Rose Buhari's haunting . . . The seemingly infinite reasons why her soul might have been trapped on the Earthly Plane seemed overwhelmingly hopeless.

Jake left the bedroom and found himself on the landing. Stairs led down to darkness, the boarded-up windows on the ground floor barely letting in any light. He took a tentative step down and his foot went through a rotten floorboard, causing him to stumble forward.

He fumbled desperately for the bannister,

momentarily relieved to find it intact, but then, with a splitting sound, the bannister cracked and he was falling. Falling into the blackness.

That's when he saw something. Or nothing. It was hard to explain, as though he was watching himself from the bottom of the stairs. Except it wasn't him – it was Rose. She was standing at the top of the steps – steps that weren't rotten and collapsing. The house wasn't derelict, either. It was how it must have been all those years ago – neat and tidy, the wallpaper no longer faded and peeling. And then he saw the figure appear behind her.

Jake tried to shout a warning from the bottom of the stairs but the cry caught in his throat.

Then the shadowed figure gave a shove.

And Rose stumbled and fell from the top all the way to the bottom of the stairs, before landing on the hard kitchen floor. Her body remained still.

Jake squeezed his eyes shut, then opened them again. The vision had faded, the house was derelict once more and he was lying on his back, with his legs over his head, at the bottom of the stairs.

But the memories of what he'd just seen were as clear if he'd been there that fateful day.

He'd seen Rose Buhari fall.

And someone had pushed her.

ZORRO

I have witnessed a murder, Jake thought.

He shook his head.

I have witnessed a murder that happened a long time ago.

He didn't know which was more shocking: the fact of the murder or the fact that he'd witnessed something that had happened before he had even been born.

He was just processing that thought when a shadow flitted across the kitchen.

Jake scrambled to his feet.

'Is there anybody there?' He reached into his pocket for his phone and switched on the torch.

'No one special, boy,' came Stiffkey's voice from the shadows. He stepped into the light. 'It's darker than my grave down here,' he said, brushing some dirt from the rim of his hat and placing it back on his head.

'Why would you do that?!' said Jake, struggling for breath. 'You scared me half to death. You could've warned me!'

Stiffkey brushed some more dirt from his waistcoat. 'When you walk through walls, there ain't no telling where you're going to end up.'

'Where's Cora?' asked Jake.

'Well, she was being impertinent again, so I left her trophy in the van and luckily she can't reach as far as the house. I left her complaining just the other side of the hedge,' said Stiffkey.

'That's a bit mean,' said Jake, smirking.

Stiffkey removed his hat and inspected it for nothing in particular. 'Anyway, boy. I come with news of Rose Buhari—'

'Murdered, I know,' finished Jake.

'That ain't what I was going to say.' Stiffkey's eyes narrowed. 'How do you know she were murdered?'

'I . . . um, I think I had . . .' started Jake, embarrassed to finish his sentence. 'I had a vision.

I saw it . . . I saw someone push Rose down the stairs. We need to find her murderer so she can be Undone.'

Stiffkey's face looked grave indeed. 'Well, boy, seems you do have those ghostly ways, whether you like it or not. Best keep that kind of thing to yourself, mind. It's known in our world as farsight . . . And farsight's Old Magic.' His brow furrowed. 'And, as you know, Old Magic is forbidden – and rightly so.'

Jake nodded. It seemed better to agree and he had no idea if the vision was real – maybe he'd hallucinated through lack of sleep? – or if it would happen again. 'What were you going to say?' asked Jake. 'If it wasn't that she was murdered.'

'It's worse than murder, boy. Well for us anyway. Rose Buhari's already been Undone!'

Stiffkey redirected Jake's phone torch around the room and there, on the wall above a rusty old sink, scrawled in red spray paint, was the symbol of the Embassy of the Dead and the initials ES.

'Edward Stapleton,' said Stiffkey. 'He's an Undoer I used to know. Not sure if he's still in the business but it seems he's Undone this ghost at some point in time. The mark's carved on to the garden gate too. Not sure how we missed it.'

'So what do we do now?' asked Jake, staring at the mark and feeling panic rise. Edward Stapleton might as well have written: *Jake Green is going to get sent to the Eternal Void.*

He didn't want to think about what this meant, but it was time to face up to things. Time to turn themselves in to the Embassy. Maybe, just maybe, there was still hope that the Embassy would help, and protect them from Mawkins, once the finger was safe.

Jake shone his torch around the kitchen again, looking for a quick way out. The sooner they left this house the better. His eyes settled on the front door. He tried the handle, even though he knew it was padlocked from the outside. A large flap had been cut in the bottom of the door. Like a home-made cat flap, but bigger, although too small for Jake to crawl through. On the floor next to the door was a ceramic bowl. A single word surrounded with hand-painted flowers read: *Zorro.*

The word was familiar from his Spanish lessons. What was it again?

El gato negro – the black cat.

El ratón blanco – the white mouse.

El zorro rojo – the red fox.

That's it! Zorro *means* fox . . .

Jake thought back to the little creature that had been watching him from the front garden.

Then something made him look up. It was the sense of something . . . A sadness. A ghost.

'Something's here,' said Jake. 'I think the Embassy missed something.' He shivered. It was cold – like when he was in the assembly hall looking for Cora.

He crouched down, pushed open the flap in the door and peered through. There on the lawn, just outside the door, sat the fox.

It was staring sadly at Rose Buhari's house.

Zorro: the ghost fox.

Jake smiled as everything clicked into place. Zorro had been Rose's pet. A tame fox. And he'd witnessed the murder! He'd seen Rose fall! It was through his eyes that Jake had seen Rose's death.

He looked back at Stiffkey and said, 'Can we Undo a fox?'

Stiffkey looked a little bemused until Jake pointed to the lonely-looking ghost animal in Rose's back garden.

Stiffkey shook his head. 'I don't know about that. Truth be told, I don't know anyone who ever tried. You certainly wouldn't get an Undoer's licence for it. Ain't you content meddling in the affairs of the human dead? Got to start meddling in the affairs of vermin, too?'

Zorro still sat in the field, gazing at the house with sorrowful eyes.

'Can't we help him at all? He seems so sad,' said Jake, beckoning for the fox to come over.

Warily, the fox trotted towards them, nervously stepping through the flap and sniffing at Jake's fingers. Its muzzle disappeared through his hand. The fox jumped back in confusion.

Stiffkey lifted his top hat and scratched his forehead. 'I've known a fair few animal ghosts - usually dogs, or ravens - the cleverer of the beasts. The others don't *feel* enough and just pass on simply.' He pulled a face. 'Never seen a ghost cat, that's for sure.' A look of disapproval crossed his face. 'Naturally self-centred creatures, cats. Wouldn't catch a cat mourning the body of its owner. Most likely eat the poor soul.'

'But surely we can Undo this one, if he's trapped and suffering?' said Jake.

'Well, the problems that trap animal ghosts on the Earthly Plane are simpler, but it's the simple problems that are the hardest to Undo. Take this fox, for example. Died of a broken heart, most likely. And the only way to fix that is to bring back Rose Buhari, which is impossible. So our young fox is going to have to wait till his energies all fade away. Just like old Stiffkey here.' He crouched down next to Jake, who was scratching the little ghost fox behind his ear, and gave the sad animal a pet too. 'Now come on, boy.' He looked at Jake from under his heavy grey eyebrows, his expression laden with sorrow. 'We need to get to the Embassy. It's time to face the music.'

Jake smiled weakly and stood up. He knew it was the right thing to do. 'Let's hope the music isn't a funeral march,' he said, bending to give the fox a last pet goodbye.

Stiffkey and Jake walked back to the van in silence. So far it had all felt unreal, almost fun at times. A crazy adventure – severed fingers, ghosts, reapers, . . . Jake could hardly believe it all himself, even after everything he'd been through. But now with every step he felt a deep fear start to take hold. And he knew he had to call Mum and Dad soon, but what would he say? How could they possibly understand what had happened to him? How could anybody? All he could do would be to say goodbye . . . He glanced down at the phone in his hand and started tapping a group message to Mum and Dad.

Hi Mum and Dad. I just needed to say

He paused. He wanted to write: *I just needed to say thanks for everything you've done for me. I love you.*

But he couldn't. Something stopped him. Something inside him that made it almost impossible to put his feelings down in words. His mind wandered to that day when Dad had left. Jake put the phone back in his pocket.

A rustling sound behind him made Jake turn round. It was the fox. It was padding behind them as they made their way back across the garden.

Jake crouched down and held out his hand. 'It's all right, boy,' he said, 'you'll be OK.' Jake scratched it comfortingly behind the ear. 'I'm sure you won't be waiting for too much longer.'

But it hurt Jake to leave the little creature there all alone. He turned to look up at Stiffkey, his eyes wide and pleading.

The old ghost stared back sternly. 'Don't even think about it, boy.' He shook his head firmly. 'Absolutely not . . . Don't we have enough troubles?'

Five minutes later, one grumpy Spectre, a furious Possessor, a grinning boy and a very happy ghost fox were all piled into the campervan, making their way to whatever fate might greet them at the Embassy of the Dead.

In the back, on the folded-down bed, lay Stiffkey. His legs fading through the closed door of the campervan, his top hat resting on his chest.

'I'll be needing to close my eyes,' said the ghost. 'If you follow the directions I gave you, we should be there in an hour or two. Please be alerting me when we arrive.'

Jake nodded. Even ghosts needed to rest, it seemed – not to sleep, exactly, just to take some time to allow their minds to still and their energies to gather. And Stiffkey needed to be strong to face the Embassy. Jake could see the worry on the old ghost's face at the thought of returning to the Embassy in disgrace – the rule-breaker – and facing judgement for interferring in the Embassy's business.

Cora sat in the front with Jake, the happy ghost fox on her lap, while Jake chewed gratefully on the cheese sandwich he'd remembered was in his rucksack. It wasn't bad considering it was two days old. He was glad his passengers were all ghosts and he didn't have to share it as, along with a Twix and a packet of crisps that made up his packed lunch, it was the only thing he'd eaten since tea with Dad. He shook his head at the thought of what his mum would say. No vegetables! Jake smiled sadly. What he wouldn't give now for one of his dad's fried breakfasts.

'Would your dad be angry if he knew you had his van?' said Cora, as if reading his thoughts.

Jake imagined his dad's reaction. 'Not angry. Upset. He's not really the angry type. What are yours like?'

Cora stared ahead. 'I don't like my parents,' she said bluntly. She turned to Jake and raised an eyebrow at him. Like she was challenging him to say something back.

He didn't. He wanted to. He wanted to ask her more about her life and her parents, but instead he changed the subject.

'It's getting colder, isn't it,' he said, embarrassed at his own awkwardness.

'Yeah. It's the fog,' said Cora, peering out of the window. 'What is it with this fog, anyway? It was sunny just a second ago.'

Jake's blood ran cold. *First the fog . . .*

Stiffkey sat up straight, fresh dirt falling from his shoulders. 'Fog, you say? I ain't keen on fog. Hides all manner of things.'

Cora pointed out the front windscreen. 'Like those two massive dogs!'

Jake pulled the wheel hard to the left, bumping on to a side track that ran behind a line of trees parallel to the road. He braked suddenly as the track faded into woodland. The engine stalled and cut out. 'It's a dead end.' He peered through the fog and saw more creatures approaching.

Cora frowned. 'Those aren't dogs!'

'Bonewulf!' shouted Jake, desperately trying to start Pickle. Nothing.

Stiffkey's head appeared by his side. 'Drive, boy! Drive!'

Jake tried again.

Still nothing.

'Come on!' cried Jake in desperation, as he turned the key in the ignition once more, but Pickle resolutely refused to start. He closed his eyes in frustration, took a deep breath to steady his nerves, then opened his eyes, ready to try again.

He immediately wished he hadn't . . .

Twenty yards ahead of them, illuminated in the full beam of the van's headlights and flanked by two more slavering bonewulf stood a tall, hooded figure, his arm outstretched, his finger pointing at Jake.

Stiffkey's voice broke the silence. 'Mawkins,' he whispered.

MAWKINS

For Jake, seeing a ghost for the first time had been something of a shock.

Seeing something that had never been alive – a creature of the Afterworld – was far worse. Even the fog seemed to wither away from him, leaving an aura of darkness that surrounded his person. His face was shadowed by a large hood and his dark robes shone with silver starlit threads, a spider web of intricate symbols and runes that changed with every slight movement of his body. But it was what hung from his neck that drew Jake's attention. There, swinging from a necklace as thick as rope, was a dead white hare.

Once again Stiffkey was first to break the horrified silence in the campervan. Still whispering at first, 'I ain't afraid.'

Then louder. 'I ain't afraid!'

He stood up and his translucent head and shoulders disappeared through the top of the van. He was shouting now . . . 'You can take my existence, Mawkins, but I won't let you take these children! They ain't done nothing wrong!'

Mawkins raised his hands out in front of him. From between them a wind blew – a sudden, ceaseless spinning breath that sucked up the loose sticks and leaves and cycloned them around the campervan, rocking it on its suspension and pulling Stiffkey up through the roof and into the air, then hurling him to the ground, where he landed in an awkward heap.

'Stiffkey!' cried Jake, flinging open the door and running towards his friend, ignoring the buffeting winds and debris. A large branch struck him on the side of the head and he stumbled and fell face down into the dirt, next to Stiffkey. One of Pickle's hubcaps flew past his head, ripped from the van by the wind. It was as though they were in the eye of a hurricane.

Mawkins, too, was inside the swirling storm,

walking slowly towards them and, with every step, the strength of the wind increased.

Beside Jake, among the dead leaves, lay Stiffkey. The old ghost's baggy eyes looked across into his.

'Mawkins wants the box and then he'll take our souls,' he gasped, struggling to breathe. 'There's no way out now. You make your peace, boy.'

'With who?'

Stiffkey smiled. 'You'll know who at the end.' He closed his eyes.

'Stiffkey? Please don't give up . . .' Jake whispered, angry tears brimming in his eyes.

'Leave us alone!' shouted Jake, a fury rising up in him.

'Yeah – leave them alone!' It was Cora.

Jake looked back over his shoulder and there she stood, brandishing her hockey stick, with Zorro yapping madly beside her.

Mawkins took another step towards them. A scythe, taller than the reaper himself, materialised in his hands and he swung it in a huge arc, slicing the air before him, opening it like a wound in the night and revealing the entrance to a tunnel.

A tunnel that led to the Eternal Void. An invisible force started to pull Stiffkey towards it . . .

Jake grabbed at Stiffkey's ankle with both hands, straining at the edge of the dark tunnel. Jake groaned with the effort – he didn't know how much longer he could hold on.

Stiffkey's eyelids fluttered open. 'Is that you, Sidney?'

'It's me, Jake,' said Jake through gritted teeth. 'You need to fight back!'

Cora leaped into action, grasping Stiffkey's leg and pulling with all her strength, while Zorro growled at the dark figure approaching.

The wrench towards the Void quickened. Jake felt the force clutching him now, too. It was like the very air around his body was clawing at him . . .

'Let go, Cora! Take Zorro . . . I can't hold on any more. Please . . . go!' Jake stared into the eyes of his friend, pleading with her to save herself.

'*Laborare pugnare parati simus!*' Cora shouted.

'Is that a magic spell?' said Jake.

'No, it's the Bodelean school motto – *We're ready to fight!* And, besides, Sanderfords never quit!'

Jake smiled even as he felt himself slipping, slipping, closer and closer towards the sucking Void . . . He shut his eyes and thought of his parents. He wished he'd finished that message . . .

'DESIST!' A loud voice cut through the screaming wind.

Jake opened his eyes and saw a man crouching in front of him, his arm held high, using the hubcap as a shield. In his other arm he held a thick, twisted stick with a dead crow taped to the end.

The man looked back at Jake and gave him a wink. 'Don't worry, kid, the cavalry's here!' he shouted over the roaring gale.

'Watch out!' cried Jake.

Out of the man's field of view, a bonewulf had crept into position, ready to attack. The man spun round and braced himself against the ground, shifting his position at the last second, deflecting the bonewulf's charge with the hubcap and sending the cadaverous beast tumbling over itself.

'Thanks, kid! I owe you!'

Now a second bonewulf pawed the ground, preparing to strike.

'DESIST!' cried the man again.

Jake felt the force of the wind momentarily weaken.

'Pull, Cora! yelled Jake.

The hold had weakened but not enough.

Zorro barked, bounding over and taking the end of Stiffkey's trouser leg in his mouth. Together, the three of them hauled with everything they had. Finally, the deadly grip released the old ghost and they tumbled backwards, landing in a heap.

Mawkins had taken a step closer to the man. Now the force of the Void was concentrated against him. The man staggered to his feet, holding his stick aloft before thrusting it firmly into the ground, like a polar explorer fighting against a blizzard to be the first to plant his flag.

'I SAID DESIST!'

And just like that the wind died and the swirling Void disappeared. Mawkins was gone. And all that was left of the bonewulf were the decomposing piles of flesh from the dead animals they had used to create their form.

The man straightened, pulled the stick

from out of the ground and walked over to the heap of boy and ghosts, who began to untangle themselves.

'Well, what do you know!' said the man with a wide, gleaming smile. 'It worked! First time. I knew I was good, but even I'm impressed!'

There was a stunned silence before Stiffkey spoke. 'Have you got a licence for using that kind of magic?'

The man glanced at Jake. 'Is he always so enthusiastically grateful? I'm blushing.'

Jake guessed the man's age to be about thirty – definitely younger than his dad but older than Sab's cousin, who was twenty-five. He wore a suit jacket over a white T-shirt, with black jeans and trainers. An expensive-looking watch glinted on his wrist. He had short hair and the sort of face that you felt you'd seen before, quite good-looking, except for a dent in his nose near the top, like it had been broken a long time ago.

'Thank you,' stuttered Jake.

'Just doing my job, saving souls one way or another,' replied the man. 'And talking of which, we can't stand here chatting all day as I for one don't want to be around when the impasse spell runs out and Mawkins returns.' He looked at the dead crow ruefully. 'Shame I couldn't find an eagle, really. That's what the spell book says. Still, not everyone has a natural ability to think fast and use their initiative, right?' He reached into his pocket and pulled out a roll of tape, twirling it around his finger.

Stiffkey shook his head. 'Old Magic is outlawed these days – who be you to be breaking the laws of the Embassy?'

'Well, I like that! That's some thanks for saving your skin!' The man laughed.

Cora picked up her hockey stick. 'I didn't ask to be saved,' she said flatly.

The man looked Cora up and down. 'My, my! A Possessor! Very interesting. 'They tend to be a little . . . temperamental.' He winked at Jake. 'You're picking up quite a gang here, Jake. First an undertaker, then a schoolgirl, and now a fox !'

Jake gave the shaking Zorro a comforting rub behind the ears.

'Who are you?' Jake said. 'And how do you know my name?'

The man smiled. 'Pleased to make your acquaintance,' he said, holding out his hand. 'I'm Goodmourning.'

OLD MAGIC

Jake looked at the business card Goodmourning had given him when they sat down in the cafe to eat a massive bowl of fries. On one side, in glossy black ink, printed on matte black, was the now familiar symbol he'd come to recognise – the three horizontal lines and three vertical lines that made up the logo of the Embassy of the Dead.

Underneath the symbol, embossed in black were the words: Agent Goodmourning, Undoer.

Jake felt bad for Cora, Zorro and Stiffkey stuck in the van but, like Goodmourning had said, it wasn't safe for ghosts to enter the cafe. Unlikely as it was that that anybody in there might be sensitive to the presence of ghosts, it was better to be safe than sorry. Besides, ghosts didn't need fries like humans did.

Goodmourning had insisted on driving. 'You're a pretty talented kid, I'm sure, but some of us are still alive –' He winked at Stiffkey, who frowned in response – 'and I for one hope to stay that way.'

As he drove, Goodmourning had explained that when Stiffkey hadn't shown up in the alleyway, he'd notified the Embassy, who told him Mawkins was already tracking the box, and Jake. Goodmourning was asked to lead the investigation into who Jake was and who he was working for. After determining Jake posed no threat to the Embassy and that his interception of the box was an honest mistake, Goodmourning requested that if was able to get to Jake before Mawkins, he be allowed to bring him in unharmed.

Jake felt his heart lift when Goodmourning told him that the Embassy had decided to make an exception to the rules, granting Jake, Stiffkey and Cora a pardon. They were no longer condemned to the Eternal Void, but they had been summoned to the Embassy so that the Ambassador could question them herself. Nothing to worry about – just a formality. And, once they were in the Embassy and the finger had been returned, Mawkins would stand down.

'It ain't like the Embassy to bend the rules,' Stiffkey had said. 'Even if they do believe we didn't mean no harm.'

Goodmourning smiled and wafted Stiffkey's concerns away. 'The Ambassador herself asked me to personally tell you, Stiffkey, that your loyalty has been recognised and appreciated, and she knows you would never purposely break a rule,' he said earnestly. 'No ghost has been a truer and more upstanding servant to the Embassy than you, and for that you deserve a second chance. Lucky old Stiffkey!'

Now Jake was happily scoffing more fries as more questions formed.

'So, if you're an Undoer, where's your ghost partner?' he asked.

'She's off on some other business at the moment,' said Goodmourning, taking a sip from his coffee. 'So you know about Undoing, do you?'

Jake nodded and picked up a handful of fries.

'And you know about Fenris and the finger?'

Jake nodded again.

'I'm so sorry you've been dragged into this,' said Goodmourning. 'You have been incredibly brave and resilient. If you were my kid, I'd be one proud parent.' He bumped Jake's fist with his. 'Why don't you pass the box to me to look after now? You've done more than your duty already.' Goodmourning smiled broadly and reached for Jake's rucksack.

Jake instinctively held it a little closer to him. 'Stiffkey says that it needs to be me that hands it over to the Embassy.' He switched to an impression of Stiffkey. 'Them that digs the holes must fill 'em.'

Goodmourning gave a thin laugh. 'Stiffkey's certainly a stickler for the rules, isn't he!' He looked around, and lowered his voice. 'I just want you to be safe, that's all. It's a dangerous time, both here on the Earthly Plane and in the Afterworld. Forces close to Fenris are gaining power, but they lack a leader . . . and a finger. If they find them, all hell will break loose –' he leaned forward – 'quite literally.' Goodmourning held a hand up in the air to attract the waitress's attention. 'You think *Mawkins* is scary?' he said. 'He's one of the good guys!'

Jake swallowed, his mouthful of fries sticking in his throat.

Goodmourning smiled as the waitress arrived. 'More fries, please! Hungry hero, here!' he added, gesturing towards Jake.

Jake felt his cheeks redden. 'Hero? Hardly. It wasn't me that saved the day out there, it was you.'

Goodmourning shook his head. 'Listen, it isn't every day a kid saves the world. That's what you've done, keeping that finger safe from whoever Rayburn is working for.'

'Oh, you know him too?' asked Jake.

'My job is to know everything around here, kid.' Goodmourning took another sip of his drink, and grimaced. 'For example, I know that this is not good coffee.' He pushed the mug away.

'Listen, kid, those powers you told me about ... those skills ... You can see ghosts, you've stood up to dangerous spirits. There aren't many that can do all that without any kind of training.' He paused then shook his head.

'Training?' said Jake. 'But I thought Old Magic was outlawed by the Embassy?'

'Well, you're right . . . It is dangerous. Maybe too dangerous for a little boy.'

'Well, I didn't say . . .' started Jake through a mouthful of fries, wanting to know more.

'You're right. It's not fair. You're just a kid. I was only thinking . . .'

'Tell me!' said Jake eagerly.

Goodmourning smiled. 'You know what? Why not . . . I was just thinking, if you want to know how to mould your gifts into true powers, I could, you know, teach you how to take advantage of your skills. I could teach you some of the –' he dropped his voice to a whisper – '*Old Magic.*'

Jake's jaw dropped.

Goodmourning smirked. 'Close your mouth when you're eating, kid. You're more disgusting than a bonewulf.'

Jake blushed.

Goodmourning smiled. 'Ignoring your table manners, all I'm saying is . . . you've got potential. And while it's true what Stiffkey says – that in some parts of the Embassy – Old Magic is frowned upon, that's not the case everywhere. Let's face it, there's a lot that old Stiffkey doesn't know about the Embassy – he's been retired a long time. Things change.' He took a fry from Jake's bowl, dipped it in ketchup. 'Stick with me, kid. Who knows, with your natural ability and my experience as the Embassy's greatest Undoer, maybe we could save the world?'

THE EMBASSY OF THE DEAD

The road to the Embassy was narrow and endless and wound its way across a bleak moor. There were no streetlights, no houses for miles. In the darkness, the campervan's headlights picked out the road in front of them and the stone wall that edged it, but nothing more. The passengers were silent, all consumed by their own thoughts.

Suddenly, a white creature loomed in their path, appearing out of the blackness ahead. Goodmourning braked abruptly and Jake lurched forward, his heart in his mouth.

A sheep was standing motionless on the road, blocking their way.

Zorro hopped on to the front of the dashboard and snarled at the woolly beast.

'It's OK, Zorro. It's just a sheep,' said Jake, with a sigh of relief, scratching the fox behind the ears.

Goodmourning beeped the horn and edged closer, until the sheep reluctantly squeezed through a gap in the stone wall and disappeared.

The campervan drove on, winding steadily through the darkness, until Goodmourning turned off on to a farm track that climbed steeply uphill. A couple of times the van failed to get enough traction and its wheels spun in the loose gravel. Eventually, though, the track levelled out at the top of the hill and then continued down over the other side, dropping into a wooded valley.

It started to rain, a flash downpour that ran along the ruts of the track, forcing Goodmourning to drive even more slowly.

Up ahead, the headlights of the campervan illuminated a wooden sign that pointed from the lane down another dark track that seemed to lead deeper into the wood.

'Wistman's Lodge,' read Goodmourning. 'Ain't far now.'

'And look!' Cora said. 'The mark! The mark of

the Embassy of the Dead is written over the sign! Can you see it, Jake?'

Goodmourning slowed the van so Jake could look properly.

Jake peered through the gloom at the sign. 'What, like the one on the box?' He blinked. 'I can't see it.'

Stiffkey grunted. 'You might be sensitive but you ain't *that* gifted, Jake. When signs are meant for ghosts only they be harder to see. And you, as a member of the unlicensed living, be looking in entirely the wrong way for a hidden thing. You be looking for something in particular, rather than for nothing at all, but us ghosts and the things us ghosts like to hide are made of exactly that. Nothingness.'

'Right . . .' said Jake. 'So if I look for nothing then I'll see something?'

Goodmourning smiled. 'Exactly! It takes a while to train your eyes to see something that isn't there. But I'm sure you'll learn quickly. You've got talent.'

Cora pulled a pretending-to-vomit face.

'Why don't you try again?' urged Goodmourning.

'I don't see why he needs to see the sign. What we need is to get there,' grumbled Stiffkey.

But Jake ignored him and tried again. First he squinted at it. Then he tried to focus in the distance past the sign. Nothing. Then he closed his eyes.

It was dark.

He opened them and his cheeks flushed as he found the others looking at him, Goodmourning raising an eyebrow and Cora shaking her head in amusement. 'Embarrassing for you,' she said.

Goodmourning leaned across and ruffled Jake's hair before driving off again. 'You still need to keep your eyes open, kid, even to see nothing. You'll pick it up! Now,' he said, pulling to a halt at a closed farm gate, 'out you get. This jacket is from Savile Row and it's pretty muddy out there.' He winked.

Jake opened the van door and looked down at the deep mud.

'Fine, but this is me paying you back for saving my life. We're even now!'

Goodmourning laughed warmly and nodded in agreement.

Jake jumped out of the van with a squelch

underfoot, slamming the door behind him. Hoodie up and head bowed against the rain, he scraped open the gate. It was only then he looked up.

Before him stood a building. Or rather, it had been a building once. A grand building. Now Wistman's Lodge was in ruins, and, through its window frames, Jake could see the night sky where long ago the roof must've been.

The campervan drove through the gate, mud splattering up Jake's jeans. He hopped back in and they drove on towards the ruins, pulling up round the back of the building where Jake saw an overgrown path leading into the dark woods beyond.

'The Embassy of the Dead . . .' said Stiffkey from the back seat. He took his hat off and bowed slightly. '*We swear to protect the living from the dead and the dead from the living and uphold the laws that keep their worlds apart.*'

'It's creepy, isn't it?' said Jake.

Stiffkey frowned. 'There ain't nothing to be scared of at the Embassy of the Dead, boy. The Embassy be representing the forces of good.'

Jake nodded. Something someone had told him once sprang into his head.

'Don't get hung up on this "good versus evil" garbage. In real life, and death, there's few that's simply one way or the other.'

It hadn't seemed like a warning. Was Mr Sixsmith talking about himself? Or was he talking about the Embassy?

Goodmourning turned to Jake. 'Now we're safely here, shall I take the box off your hands? I would be happy to deliver it to the Ambassador on your behalf, save you the earache she'll give you. She's quite a formidable woman.' He smiled at Cora. 'I guess Jake's used to that, though.'

Cora snarled.

Jake felt a burden being lifted. He'd brought the finger all this way, surely Goodmourning could now take the box. 'Yes, I guess that would be fine now we—' he began, reaching into his bag as he spoke, but Stiffkey's hand shot forward, pushing the box back into Jake's bag and interrupting.

'Remember, Jake,' said Stiffkey, looking into his eyes, 'the one who digs the hole fills it. And now is not the time to be breaking more Embassy rules.' He turned to Goodmourning with a frown. 'Surely you know that only Jake can take the box inside?'

Jake sighed. He'd almost gotten rid of the Damned Thing. A strange look flashed across Goodmourning's face, then he smiled. 'You do like to play by the book, don't you?! Personally, I would say that particular rule is more about honour than something to be taken literally . . .'

Stiffkey looked shocked. 'And do you think now is the time to be dishonouring the Embassy?'

'You're absolutely right,' said Goodmourning. He seemed to think for a moment. Then he turned to Jake and placed his hands on his shoulders. 'I tell you what, kid, why don't you sit tight in the van while me and Stiffkey go and get us an appointment with the Ambassador?'

'OK,' Jake replied.

'It ain't safe to leave the boy out here alone,' said Stiffkey, taking a step closer to Jake.

'Don't worry, he'll be fine. Mawkins will be hours behind the scent. You know an unlicensed member of the living can't just walk into the Embassy – I'll have to get a permit. We'll be five minutes, tops.'

Stiffkey nodded reluctantly.

Goodmourning reached into his pocket and retrieved his phone. 'One second!' He tapped out a quick message.

'What about me?' asked Cora.

Goodmourning picked up Cora's trophy. 'You can come with us,' he said, shutting the lid of the trophy.

Cora vanished.

'She won't like that,' said Jake.

'I'll take the heat, don't you worry,' said Goodmourning with a wink. 'See you soon, promise.'

Jake watched as his friends disappeared through the rain into the ruins.

He breathed a sigh of relief.

Mawkins would go back to the Afterworld.

It was nearly over.

He'd soon be home.

And yet . . .

And yet something didn't *feel* right.

He looked at Zorro, who had been curled up asleep on the driver's seat. He was sitting up now.

Ears pricked. Alert. His lip curled back into the beginnings of a snarl.

There was something outside, its reflection caught in the wing mirrors of the campervan. At first Jake saw a small dark shape slowly approaching, then the clouds thinned. Jake could make out the figure of a man with a bandaged head, stooping against the rain. It was the man from Cora's school. It was Rayburn. He had come for the box.

RAYBURN AGAIN

Jake was trapped – frozen in fear – and with every step Rayburn took it became increasingly unlikely that Jake could escape.

Think, think . . .

And then it came to him. Rayburn wasn't really looking for a finger, or even for Jake.

He was looking for a box.

And he too would be under strict instructions not to open it.

But there was no other option. Jake couldn't let him find the finger. The terrifying image of Mawkins flashed into his mind. Jake pushed it away.

Quickly, he reached for his rucksack, and clamouring over into the back, he lay on the grubby floor and hid himself beneath the seats, Zorro jumping down there with him. As fast as he could,

Jake unzipped his rucksack and took out the box. Then, feeling for the brass clasp with a shaking hand, he took a deep breath and opened it.

Gritting his teeth in the darkness, he reached through the ripped newspaper and clutched the finger. It was the first time he'd touched it. It was smooth, where the skin had tightened around the knuckles, then rough at the neatly severed end. Fighting a gag reflex, he quickly wrapped it in a napkin from the service station cafe and stuffed it back into his pocket. Then he closed the lid.

But as he held the box it felt wrong. It felt empty. He looked around for something, anything, to put in the box to replace the finger, but in the darkness of the van he could neither see nor feel anything to use. He reached again into his pocket. There, nestling beside the napkin-wrapped severed finger of a long-dead composer possessed by one of the Twelve Reapers of the Afterworld, was his precious mobile phone.

He could hear Rayburn's footsteps crunch on the gravel outside the van. With only seconds left, he quickly placed his phone into the box, covered it with the newspaper and shoved it into his rucksack. Then he zipped the bag back up and tossed it in between the front seats. Finally, he pulled Dad's big waxed jacket down from the seat above to cover him and Zorro, and lay in the dark, his heart pounding.

Just in time.

There was a loud rattle right by Jake's head. The sound of someone trying the door at the back of the van. To Jake's relief, it was locked.

Then there was a click – the sound of someone having more luck with the driver's door. It opened and the van swayed as the large man climbed aboard.

There was a triumphant grunt.

He'd found the bag!

He heard the man muttering and the sound of the zip being opened. It went quiet for a moment.

'Hello,' said Rayburn.

Jake held his breath.

'. . . he's not here.'

Jake breathed out quietly. Rayburn was talking on a phone. Jake could faintly hear a voice on the other end of line.

'Nope,' said Rayburn gruffly, 'but the box is . . .

Of course I haven't opened it . . . Right, I'll meet you
at the graveyard.'

And then Rayburn stood up and climbed down
from the van, slamming the door behind him.

After a minute Jake slowly peeked out from the
jacket, Zorro sticking his nose out too. All was quiet.

Jake felt something move in his pocket. He slid
his hand in, expecting to find his phone, but then
remembered his phone was now inside a box in the
possession of the psychopathic henchman of an
unknown villain hell-bent on helping a fallen reaper
take over the Afterworld. So, if the movement wasn't
his phone, what else was in his pocket?

A sickness welled up in Jake's stomach as he
realised. The finger! He took it from his pocket and
looked at it wriggling in the palm of his hand.

It was the most stomach-churningly awful thing
he'd ever seen: a severed human finger, yellowed by
age, long since dismembered from its accompanying
body, wriggling and flexing as though it was alive –
slowly working its way out of the old napkin that
had held it, like some kind of horrific, withered grub
emerging from a papery cocoon. Its long fingernail

scratched lightly against Jake's palm as it struggled for purchase. It seemed to be seeking something . . .

Something outside the campervan.

Something evil.

Why had it started moving?

Jake was sure it hadn't done that before. But then, he'd only opened the box once before. He wrapped the finger up again in the napkin and shoved it deep into his pocket.

He needed to tell someone what he'd seen, what he'd done. He needed Goodmourning. Before Rayburn came back.

Checking no one was outside, he climbed from the van. Zorro moved to follow him.

'Stay here, Zorro. This could be dangerous. I'll be back soon.' He gave the sad-looking ghost fox a last scratch behind the ear and closed the door quietly behind him.

Taking care to keep to the shadows, Jake ran through the mud and into the Embassy of the Dead.

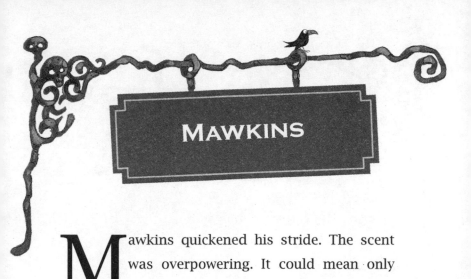

MAWKINS

Mawkins quickened his stride. The scent was overpowering. It could mean only one thing. The Damned Thing was free.

He gathered the mist around him like a cloak and sank away to nothing, into the Earth, rising again in the shadow of a ruined building: the Embassy of the Dead. Of all places!

He shook his head. He remembered a time before the Embassy. When the places where the Afterworld overlapped with the Earthly Plane were merely bridges between neighbouring lands. Things were simpler then. Fewer rules, fewer duties.

No matter. He held out his arms and the scythe grew from the darkness swirling between his hands. At least some things never changed. There were souls to be reaped.

The Cloakroom Attendant

Jake wasn't expecting anything in particular when he stepped through the doorway into the Embassy of the Dead, but he was expecting something. Not just ruins.

He was at the bottom of a large double-height reception room, a room that once must have been grand, but now patches of stars shone through the collapsed roof and shifting columns of rain fell to the cracked floor, gathering in puddles that shimmered in the moonlight.

A double staircase swept upwards to his left and right, joining again at the landing on the second floor. The stairs were broken and incomplete, shattered remnants of their former splendour.

At the foot of the stairs Jake saw the rusted grille of an ancient elevator. Beyond the grille a light caught his attention. A soft undulating electric glow that caught the dust floating in the air. Slowly he approached and peered through the grille.

His heart stopped.

A ghostly face was staring back at him from the gloom, the face of a spectral child imprisoned in the caged elevator. Dirty and messy-haired, with a look of complete terror etched across his face.

Jake blinked, and so did the boy.

'Idiot,' he muttered to himself.

It was his own reflection cast in the elevator's mirrored wall. Jake waited for his heart to slow down to a safe rate and looked through the grille again. The glow was coming from a column of buttons.

B – G̲ – 1 – 2.

He scanned the rest of the ruined building. A carcass of its former self, the roofless beams spanned the sky, as if he was standing inside the ribcage of a huge fallen skeleton. So strange that within this dead ruin there should be this single pulsing glow of light.

Jake gripped the cage doors of the elevator, pulled them open and stepped inside.

He squinted at the row of buttons.

Which one?

He remembered Stiffkey's words:

You be lookin' for something in particular, rather than for nothing at all.

What did that even mean? How did you look for nothing at all? He blinked. And there it was – appearing just as he stopped looking for it – another button above the others, marked with the triple crossed sign of the Embassy of The Dead.

Jake took a deep breath and pressed the button. A dull, flickering light suddenly lit the interior of the elevator and, with a harsh scraping sound, it began to move. Floor 1, 2 . . . and still it continued to ascend for ten seconds or so, before finally shuddering to a halt.

All was silent. The old-fashioned elevator, with its thick dusty carpet and protective grille, seemed like a sanctuary from whatever dangers might lie in wait.

Jake felt a movement in his hoodie. The finger was struggling against the paper now – trying to worm itself free. Jake clamped his hand over his pocket, fighting back the urge to retch. He could feel the finger, writhing through the fabric.

The tuneless chime of an ancient bell sounded and the elevator door slid open.

'I say! Hello there. Do come in!'

The ghost of a suited young man leaped up from an armchair facing the lift, a cocktail glass held delicately in one hand. He looked like he'd just got back from a night out in the 1920s. A white silk scarf was draped around his shoulders and an unfastened bowtie hung from his slender neck.

He paused and looked Jake up and down, shaking his head dramatically. 'I see you've not dressed for the occasion.'

He beckoned Jake into the room. 'No matter. It's your first time here, isn't it? I can tell. I'm Eustace the cloakroom attendant.' He held out his hand to Jake.

Jake looked at it suspiciously. If his encounter with Mr Sixsmith had taught him anything it was to be wary of ghostly strangers. 'I'm Jake, nice to meet you,' he said. 'I'm looking for Goodmourning.

He probably just came in? I need to see him immediately, please.'

The man smiled. 'I'm sorry but I'm not at liberty to talk about other guests here. Confidentiality and all that, I'm sure you understand . . .'

Jake frowned. 'Um, but this is very urgent. Do you think you might be able to bend the rules? I just need to know . . .'

Jake tailed off as Eustace raised an eyebrow. Whatever Goodmourning said, bending the rules was obviously not the done thing round here.

Eustace took a sip of his cocktail. 'Listen, as it's your first time, I'm going to forget you said that. I just know you're going to find whatever you need once you're inside.'

'I'm not inside yet?'

Eustace pirouetted round and, with a flourish, announced dramatically, 'The entrance to the Embassy of the Dead lies beyond.' He pointed to a thick velvet curtain.

'Thank you,' said Jake, rushing hurriedly towards the curtain.

The smile dropped from Eustace's face. 'Oh,

goodness me. Not like that, young man. I'll need to relieve you of your baggage.'

Jake scratched his head. 'What baggage?'

Eustace smiled sympathetically. 'I need to take your life.'

Jake stopped short. 'What?!' he said in a high-pitched voice.

'This is the Embassy of the Dead. You leave your life at door, thank you very much.' Eustace reached inside the curtain and flicked a switch. A light came on and Jake could see a row of trolleys, covered with sheets that seemed to be hiding body-shaped objects underneath.

'Their spirits are inside the Embassy,' Eustace explained. 'It's the only way the living can enter.'

Jake nodded as if he understood. 'Right. How do I do that?'

Eustace rolled his eyes. '*You* don't have to do it. If everybody could do it, I'd be out of a job. Allow me.'

Eustace walked behind Jake and placed his hands on his shoulders. Jake could hardly feel his touch, it was so light, but a chill ran down his back and he shivered involuntarily. Eustace leant forward so his mouth was close to Jake's ear. 'If you would take a step forward, please, young man,' he whispered. 'Et, voilà!' he said, as Jake gratefully stepped forward. 'Aren't I clever?'

Jake turned round, expecting to see Eustace standing there. He was, but someone else was standing in front of him. A scruffy boy. The same boy he'd seen reflected in the mirror. It was Jake, but he looked different somehow . . . The Jake-not-Jake was vacant and stood awkwardly, like he was about to topple over. Real Jake looked down at his hands. They were faded and transparent. He had literally stepped outside his own body and now it stood before him, like a senseless lump of bone and flesh.

Eustace was clearly proud of himself and said, 'And now for my next trick!' He stepped forward and disappeared into Jake's statue body. It was quite possibly the most alarming thing Jake had ever witnessed, and that was saying something given the unlikely direction his life had taken recently. He fought the impulse to scream as the

Jake-not-Jake danced over to the cloakroom, waving goodbye as he pulled the curtain shut behind him. A few seconds later the curtain opened again and Eustace stepped out, bowing low. 'Impressive stuff, I know! Not many ghosts can possess a living form at will. In fact there's only two of us. The less said about the other fellow the better!'

Jake peered round the curtain. There, on the closest trolley, lay his own body.

He suddenly panicked, wondering if the finger would stay with his body over there, but breathed a sigh of relief to feel its form in his pocket. It was still wriggling slightly, but didn't seem so intent on escaping.

Eustace sensed Jake relief. 'Certain objects will accompany your ghost. It depends upon your sensitivity.' He handed Jake a ticket. 'You'll need this to reclaim your suit.'

'Um, I'm not wearing a suit, just a –' Jake looked down at himself – 'um, jeans and—'

Eustace interrupted. 'Your *meat* suit, as we Bodyshifters like to call it, is your body! You can pick it up on the way out. But don't be too long or you'll end up in the graveyard out back.'

Jake felt the now-familiar feeling of alarm rise once again, but forced himself to ask calmly, 'What graveyard?'

'Wistman's Lodge used to have a chapel with a small family graveyard,' said Eustace, adding with a smile, 'which is a handy place for us to put the bodies of the living who stay too long in the Embassy!'

Jake couldn't tell if he was joking or not. 'How long is too long?'

'It's different for every living person, but you'll feel it – a sort of tug – and then you'll need to come back here,' said Eustace, suddenly looking serious. 'You'll be able to stay longer on your next visit, as your spirit acclimatises to being without its body.'

Eustace drew back the curtain fully and led Jake through. Alongside the line of trolleys ran a long corridor with a plush-looking red carpet running down the centre, at the end of which was a flight of stairs leading upwards to an ornately carved wooden door.

Eustace accompanied Jake to the door then bowed low and motioned for Jake to enter. 'Welcome to being dead!'

TEMPORARILY DEAD

As the door swung open, Jake was greeted by the sound of excited chatter. A queue of around twenty people snaked through a large, brightly lit room. It seemed impossible to Jake that this room could be inside the ruined building that he'd seen from the outside. The woman in front of him turned round. Her hair was standing on end and a wisp of smoke wound up, escaping from somewhere inside her singed boiler suit. 'I was electrocuted by a wind turbine,' she declared proudly. 'Bet they don't get too many of them.'

Jake smiled politely. It was hard to know what to say.

'Turns out you have to queue even when you're dead. Unless you're one of the lucky ones that gets

seen by an auditor at the location of their haunting.'
She handed him a leaflet. 'Did you get one of these?'

Jake took it, surprised to feel the woman's hand
against his own. In fact, he couldn't see through her
at all, or through anyone else in the queue. And his
own hand was now completely solid. Perhaps in the
Embassy all ghosts had form? He reminded himself
to ask Goodmourning about it later.

Jake scanned the cover of the leaflet. A picture
of a semi-translucent man in a cardigan, underneath
the title: *So You're a Ghost: A Guide for the Newly
Deceased.*

'You can have it. I've read it already.'

Jake handed it back to the woman, 'It's fine,
thanks. I'm actually still alive.'

The woman smiled sympathetically. 'It took me
a while to accept things too. We're all on our own
journey, aren't we?'

Jake smiled politely again. He looked over
the woman's shoulder, down the slow-moving
queue. It led to a large marble desk, behind which
a woman was talking to the ghost in front of her
while constantly tapping on a huge, ancient-looking

desktop computer. Hanging above her was a sign that read:

THE NEWLY DEAD

To the left of her was another desk, manned by a friendly-looking woman talking to a ghostly man holding a mop and bucket. She was sitting under a second sign:

EMBASSY EMPLOYEES

To the right was a third desk with no queue. Barely visible over the rim of the desk sat a small man, wearing glasses and an extremely bored expression on his face. Above him hung another sign:

THE TEMPORARILY DEAD

'Sorry, I'm in the wrong queue!' said Jake, racing forward.

The man's brow was creased in concentration as he stared at the screen in front of him.

Jake cleared his throat. 'Excuse me—'

'One moment.' The man's finger paused over the full-stop key. He didn't look up.

Jake leaned forward. 'It's an emergency!'

The man's eyes remained trained on the screen for what felt like for ever, until he pressed a final key and ripped a sheet from the printer next to him. 'How can I help you?' he said, not looking up from the paper in front of him.

'I . . .' Jake lowered his voice to a whisper. 'I need to speak to Goodmourning. It's about . . .' He paused. How best to explain that he was currently in possession of the Damned Thing? 'It's about something of –' he paused to pick the best words – 'something of a *sensitive nature.*'

'I see,' said the man, *still* not looking up.

It took a lot to push Jake over the edge. Sab often tried for hours to make him mad and then got mad himself when Jake remained relatively relaxed. Jake guessed he was more of a 'keep it bottled up on the inside' type. Probably not the healthiest way to be, he thought, as he felt the anger inside bubbling to the surface and about to explode.

'You do realise you're in the Embassy of the Dead?' said the small man.

'Yes,' said Jake through gritted teeth.

The man finally looked up, smiling smugly. '*All* of the information we deal with is of a sensitive nature.'

'It's urgent!' blurted out Jake, loudly. The chatter in the room died out and Jake felt multiple pairs of eyes turn to look at him. 'I need to find Goodmourning,' he pleaded.

The door opened behind the desk and a boy about Jake's age came out, pushing an empty cart. Jake watched as the boy switched his cart with another cart full of paperwork and went back through the door.

The man slowly stamped the piece of paper in front of him, placed it in the empty cart, then turned to Jake and said, 'If I could just take your details please . . . Licence number?'

Jake looked at him blankly.

'It's on your Undoer's Licence card.'

'Um, I lost it,' said Jake, thinking on his feet.

'Then you'll have to fill in form 12b for a

replacement card, which I'll then send to the Undoers department, who'll need a stamp of approval from Renewals and authorisation from the Ambassador, before it is returned to me and you will then receive a new licence within twenty-one to twenty-eight days, at which time you may enter the Embassy of the Dead. Now, I'll just find the correct form.' He hopped down from his chair and disappeared from view under the desk, searching in one of the drawers.

After a few minutes he reappeared with a thick wedge of paper, but Jake was no longer there and nor was the cart.

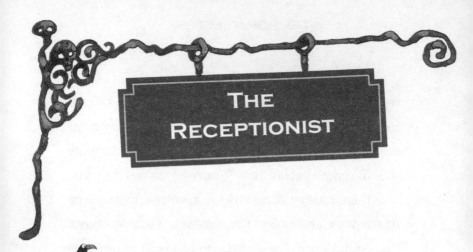

THE RECEPTIONIST

While the small man was beneath the desk, Jake had snuck around the side and grabbed the cart. It was hardly a disguise, but as he hurriedly pushed it through the door he felt some comfort that at least he had something.

He found himself in another corridor, this one lined with doors. His heart sank – he had no idea which way to go. He winced as one of the doors swung open, nearly whacking him in the face. An elderly man stomped out, muttering, 'As if ninety years weren't long enough to be alive, and now I'm stuck as a Poltergeist! All I can do is make a scratching sound. The janitor at the old folks' home thinks I'm a faulty air vent!' He looked up and redirected his rant in Jake's direction. 'It was forty years ago I last burgled. I've been straight a long time now. I wish I'd never nicked that flaming ring. But I'm a romantic and knew the wife would love it. The only way I can be Undone and stop those blimin' longings is for it to be returned to its rightful owner, but the waiting list is twelve years! You don't get that for murder these days.' He buried his head in his hand.

Jake nodded in sympathy and read the sign on the door:

COMPLAINTS

Not sure that will help. He turned and read the opposite door:

AUTHORISED PERSONNEL ONLY

That seemed a better option. Jake tried the door, expecting it to be locked, but it opened with a click. A security guard sat reading a newspaper on the other side of the door. He looked up and nodded at Jake, who smiled politely.

'Fake it till you make it,' as Sab would say, thought Jake. Sab was the king of blagging. Jake was usually the honest one. Not today, though.

He was in a busy office, with lots of desks and people on huge clunky phones. The chatter of multiple voices echoed around the room.

'I'm afraid your auditor is running late.'

'There is no appeal process available for death.'

'Hey!' A woman called at Jake from a nearby desk. 'Has the Summerfield file showed up yet?'

Jake shook his head.

The woman shrugged. 'Oh well. It's only another ten years until an Undoer becomes available again. Summerfield will just have to wait.'

Jake felt a twinge of guilt, unsure what he'd done, but he needed to keep focused. He made his way across the office floor, trying to look like he should be there.

At the far end of the office was a door that led to yet another corridor, in which Jake found, to his delight, a huge map. He searched for the 'You are here' arrow and then scanned the rest of the map, unsure of exactly what he was searching for until he found it: *Undoers' Chambers.*

Bingo.

Jake knocked on the door labelled 'Goodmourning'.

No answer.

He knocked again.

Still no answer.

He looked around the empty corridor, then tried the door. It swung open. The Embassy really needed better security.

Goodmourning's chambers were bare apart from a desk, a neatly made bed and a bedside table.

'Goodmourning?' Jake called out. 'Stiffkey? Cora?'

Jake sighed. He'd done so well to get here, but what was he supposed to do now? His cover could get blown at any moment. He suddenly felt very tired.

Jake sat on the edge of the bed, tapping his

pocket again to make sure the finger was still there. It squirmed at his touch.

He stood up and walked over to the desk, sitting behind it and swinging back on the comfortable chair. Next to the phone was a directory. He opened it up and scanned the list of numbers until he saw a name he'd heard: the Ambassador.

That's who Goodmourning was going to talk to! Maybe he was there with Stiffkey right now?

Jake picked up the phone and dialled the number quickly, waiting anxiously for it to ring. After just two rings, a voice answered. Not for the first time, Jake wished he'd mentally prepared for the conversation before picking up the phone. 'Ambassador's office, Maureen speaking. How may I be of assistance?'

'I've got a finger,' he blurted.

There was a pause on the other end of the line.

'I beg your pardon.'

'My name is Jake and I have a very important deliv—'

Jake paused as a sudden wave of nausea washed over him and he felt a sharp pain in his chest.

Almost as if something was pulling him backwards.
He remembered Eustace's warning . . .

You'll feel it . . . A sort of tug . . .

He had to get back to the cloakroom before he
became trapped as a ghost for ever.

'Hello?' came a confused, muffled voice from
the phone. 'I'm afraid the line's not very good, you'll
have to speak a little louder . . .'

'Hello, Ambassador's office? This is Jake. I
haven't got very long or I'm going to get trapped
here, but is Goodmourning there? I need to talk to
him. It's an emergency . . .'

'Hello? Goodmourning, is that you? Where on
earth have you been? We haven't heard from you
in weeks. The Ambassador is furious . . .' said the
voice at the other end of the line.

Jake let the phone drop from his mouth.

Goodmourning had said he was going straight
there. And that he'd already spoken to the
Ambassador who had pardoned them . . .

Jake was confused. And then he felt the tug
again, sharper this time . . . he couldn't have long
left.

'Look, I don't know if you can hear me, and I don't really know what's going on, but this isn't Goodmourning, this is Jake Green. I was with Goodmourning half an hour ago and he told me he was meeting the Ambassador. I've got the finger. Someone's being trying to steal it from me – the person who's stolen the body, I think – and I gave them the box instead to fool them, but it won't fool them for long and I have to . . . Hello? Hello, can you hear me?'

The line went dead.

THE FINAL COUNTDOWN

Jake doubled over as the pain tugged at his chest. He had to get out now! But which way?

He searched his jeans and pulled out the cloakroom ticket that he'd been given in exchange for his 'meat suit'. Maybe that would tell him what to do? Where before he could have sworn it had said 214, now it said 178. Had he been mistaken? He blinked as the number changed before his eyes:

It was counting down.

He turned on his heel and bolted for the door, quite literally running for his life. Abandoning the cart he'd left outside Goodmourning's room he started to retrace his steps.

The Embassy was like a maze and at some point in his rush Jake had taken a wrong turn. He stopped for breath, leaning against the wall for support. There was no time to go back. He'd never make it. He had to find a new way.

He was now in one of the building's older outer corridors, with large windows punctuating one of its walls. The rain lashed against the glass. Jake paused and peered into the darkness, feeling hopeless. Maybe this was it? Time to accept his death? But then he saw the campervan. Dad. Mum. Home. He couldn't get this far and then give up.

He ran on, glancing down at the ticket.

Time was running out.

A door opened at the far end of the corridor

and a man walked through carrying a bin-bag. He lifted a large flap in the wall and placed the bin-bag inside. Then he turned and disappeared back through the door.

'Wait!' cried Jake. He ran towards the door, flinging it open to reveal yet another corridor of doors. The cleaner was nowhere to be seen.

He went back through the door and went over to the flap in the wall. Above it was a sign that read GENERAL WASTE. It was some sort of garbage disposal chute. He opened the flap and peered down into a dark, smelly tunnel.

No way was he getting in there.

He looked at the ticket again.

Clenching his jaw, Jake wriggled, feet first, into the chute, before deciding that the whole plan was stupid. He had no idea where it led. Maybe to an incinerator?! He tried to climb, but it was too late. He was falling . . . Falling into the blackness, rattling down the metal chute. He pressed himself against the edge, using his body as a brake and, for a second, he slowed, then immediately sped up again as he fell, screaming all the way, before landing in a pile of bin-bags in a skip. A door opened, flooding the room with light.

'Well, that's a new one!' came the voice of Eustace. 'I was starting to worry about you, but I heard the screaming and here you are. Welcome back!'

Eustace took a sip from his cocktail glass and sauntered over to Jake, offering him a hand. This time Jake took it gladly and stood up, pulling himself out of the skip. He peeled something slimy off his face. *Gross.*

Eustace led Jake out of the room and straight into the trolley room. He walked over to one trolley and whipped off the sheet with a flourish, revealing the Jake-not-Jake lying motionless. Then, in the blink of an eye, Eustace disappeared and Jake's body got up from the trolley and walked over to him. Then Eustace emerged once more.

'Your vessel awaits!' he said, motioning Jake to step forward. Jake took a deep breath and stepped inside his own body. He looked at his hands.

He felt nothing. No change at all.

'I'm back in my body?' he said, patting his pocket to find the finger once more.

Eustace nodded. 'It's as simple as that! I hope you enjoyed yourself in the Embassy. You'll be able to stay longer next time.'

A screeching noise sounded through the night. Eustace walked over to a window and peered out. 'That animal! It's been screeching non-stop. Sounds like a fox or something . . . Most annoying when one's trying to relax.'

Jake gasped. *Zorro!*

He sprinted to the lift and pressed the button for the ground floor.

Eustace waved at him through the closing doors. 'So you won't be joining me for a cocktail, then?'

FOLLOW THE FINGER

Jake exploded from the Embassy, back out into the cold night air.

'Zorro!' he called. 'Zorro?' He peered into the night, hoping to see his friend come bounding through the darkness towards him. But there was no sight or sound of the fox.

He was alone. No Zorro, no Cora, no Stiffkey and no Goodmourning. Goodmourning had lied to him. He hadn't gone into the Embassy or even spoken to them for months!

Then he remembered the look that had flashed across Goodmourning's face after Stiffkey told him not to hand the box over.

How he'd sent a message before he left and how, minutes later, Rayburn had turned up, knowing just where to find Jake . . .

And the box!

How could he have been so stupid! Goodmourning was Rayburn's boss. And now Stiffkey and Cora and maybe Zorro, too, were with him and in danger . . . Jake had to find them.

Just then the finger started squirming madly in his pocket. Jake put a hand over it, feeling it flex and twist, trying to squeeze free. It was like it was seeking something out.

Jake realised what it wanted. 'The body. It's looking for its body! And if I find the body, I'll find the others . . .'

He pulled the toggle string from his hoodie. Quickly, he tied it around the middle knuckle of the finger and dangled it in the air.

The finger started to move.

He closed his eyes, wishing for it to work. Then he opened them again. The finger was twitching now – like a maggot on a hook. Then it stopped, and started to spin. A recognition of their shared aim – like it understood that they both wanted to find the body, even if for very different purposes.

Jake watched as the spinning got faster. Then,

suddenly, the finger stopped and stiffened. Not jerking or pulling but pointing away from the Embassy and into the pitch darkness of the woods beyond.

'The graveyard . . . of course,' said Jake.

The first twenty metres through the woodland were hard going, but soon he broke free of the dense scrub and found himself on a grassy track that cut through the trees. Jake held the finger aloft. It spun to the left and stopped. Now Jake was sprinting, urging his exhausted body onwards. In the distance he heard Zorro screech again. Louder this time. The finger pointed to a winding path leading downwards towards the sound of the fox's cries. Jake dived down the path, ignoring the thorns that caught in his clothes and plucked at his skin. His foot hit something hard – he stumbled and fell, tumbling down a mossy bank that ended abruptly at the top of a flint wall. Then he fell again. Down the height of the wall. His left hand instinctively shot up into the air, keeping the severed finger safe from harm, before he landed with a thud on the ground.

He pushed himself up and wiped his muddy right hand on his jeans. He was standing in an overgrown graveyard. Jake held the finger aloft once more and followed the direction it was pointing. He could see taller gravestones in the distance and tombs, too, and there, pawing at the entrance to a small moss-covered stone building, was his fox.

'Zorro!' Jake called to him and broke into a run. Zorro turned at the sound of Jake's voice and bounded over to greet his friend.

'What's in there, Zorro? Is it the others?'

Jake stared ahead at the large stone tomb. A rusting metal door in the front of it was slightly ajar.

Jake consulted the finger.

It was pointing towards the open door. Then it spun round, beckoning Jake to enter.

THE MAUSOLEUM

Jake wrapped the finger tightly in the napkin once more and placed it in his pocket. He turned back to Zorro. 'Stay,' he commanded hopefully. Zorro looked frustrated, but obediently sat on his haunches.

Jake thought about Stiffkey and Cora, how they'd both saved his life. He pulled at the edge of the metal door. It creaked as he inched it open. Taking a deep breath he began to creep down the steep stone steps that led underground, following the dim light glowing from the open arch at the bottom of the steps. It led into a small chamber with a dirt floor.

A figure stood at the edge of a freshly dug grave, leaning on his shovel, with mud on his face and hands. Stiffkey.

A look of guilt spread across the old ghost's face. 'Oh, Jake. You be a few ha'pennies short of a farthin' coming here, boy . . . You should have run once he took the finger.' Stiffkey shook his head at Jake sadly, then shouted, 'Watch yourself, boy!'

But it was too late. Rayburn had appeared behind Jake and swiftly put him in a chokehold, his thick forearm wrapped around Jake's neck. He couldn't move and could barely breathe.

'Course it wasn't Stiffkey, kid,' said another voice from the chamber.

Goodmourning. In one hand he held Cora's trophy. In the other he held the box.

'Do you really think old Stiffkey would pull off something like this? He's just trying to save the girl.' He held up Cora's trophy. 'It would be a shame if something happened to her trophy. You know what happens to a Possessor if her possession is destroyed, don't you?' Goodmourning pretended to shudder and then laughed cruelly. 'Anyway, I'm so glad you could make it to the special event. Of course, we would have been here a lot sooner if old Stiffkey had let me take the finger in the first place.

But turns out you aren't a hero, just a scared little boy, running away to hide and leaving the nasty box behind.' He shook his head and tutted at Jake. 'I thought better of you.'

Goodmourning's face hardened. 'Go and guard the entrance,' he snapped at Rayburn. 'And shut that door. We don't want any more interruptions!'

Giving Jake a final shove as he released him, Rayburn sloped off up the steps.

Jake gripped the finger tightly inside his pocket. Maybe he'd been surprised by Goodmourning's betrayal, but he still had one thing in his favour. He had the finger. And at all costs he must keep it from Goodmourning. But as soon as Goodmourning opened the box, he'd know. Jake had to keep him talking until help came, if it ever would.

He wondered if the Ambassador's office had heard any of what he said on the phone. It seemed doubtful. But Mawkins would be here soon and, even if it meant them all being sent to the Eternal Void, at least it would be better than the whole Earthly Plane being under the rule of Fenris and his followers – people like Goodmourning.

'Why don't you let Stiffkey and Cora go? This has nothing to do with them,' said Jake, his hands balling into fists.

'And have them go crying to the Embassy? I don't think so. You should all be thankful – it's not often you get to see the very moment in history where everything is tipped in the favour of what our friend Stiffkey would call *evil*. If I was you, Jake, I'd be thinking very carefully about which side you want to be on. Clue: choose the winning one. Mine.'

'I don't want to be on any side you're on!' shouted Jake.

Goodmourning shrugged. 'Shame . . . we could have used a kid of your talents. Now, enough small talk. It is time. Is the coffin safely in its final resting place?' He peered into the hole. 'Good. I trust the grave is suitable for one of his honour?'

Stiffkey nodded. 'I ain't never dug a bad grave before and I don't intend to dig one now, even if it's for a purpose with which I am not agreeing. You be doing an evil thing and you'll face the consequences when the Embassy catch up to you.'

'Oh, I shouldn't think so. Once Fenris is back

in charge, I rather think he'll do away with the Embassy and their outdated rules altogether, and I shall be richly rewarded for my efforts in bringing about the new order.'

Jake reached out to the old ghost. 'I'm sorry, Stiffkey. I thought for a moment . . .' he trailed off, feeling terrible.

Stiffkey smiled sadly. 'It don't matter now, boy. Don't you be troubling yourself.' He glared at Goodmourning. 'It's you who will be troubled when all your wickedness catches up with you.'

Goodmourning frowned and raised a palm towards Stiffkey. He uttered some words. Strange words that Jake didn't understand.

Stiffkey dropped his shovel and fell to the ground, as though struck hard in the chest. 'You ain't allowed to do that,' he said, gasping for breath.

'Old Magic, Stiffkey. It's incredibly powerful once you learn how to master it!' Goodmourning laughed. 'It's time for the crimes of the past to be undone and the new master of the dead and the living to rise!'

'How did you even find the body?' asked Jake.

He had to try to keep Goodmourning talking, delay the moment when he'd realise the finger was missing. 'Didn't the Embassy have it hidden somewhere impossible to discover?'

Goodmourning looked at Jake and a smug smile spread over his face.

'Finding the body was easy. It only took fifteen years' loyal service to the Embassy before I reached a high enough level of security clearance to access the file. But time is of no importance in the grand scheme of the power about to be freed. Patience is its own weapon.' He paused, seeming to allow himself a moment of appreciation. 'Of course the body was going to be in the Embassy's own graveyard. And where? An unmarked spot. A pauper's grave?' He snarled in disgust. 'The body Fenris chose deserves a grander tomb, no?' He motioned at the vaulted chamber. 'And who at the Embassy would be clever enough to guess its new location – the very same graveyard where it was originally hidden!'

He stared at Jake, waiting for a response.

'Er, yup. Definitely,' said Jake. It seemed wise not to disagree.

'The finger was harder to find,' Goodmourning continued. He was pacing around the little cavern now, waving his arms about as he told his story. 'Three years I searched for it, trying to work out which agent was hiding it and where. I hadn't even considered Stiffkey, as we all thought he'd retired. A clever ruse, leaving it with an old has-been.' He gave Stiffkey a wink that made Jake's blood boil. But at least he was talking. Jake glanced up at the doorway again, but still no one came.

'And then it came to me – a flash of inspiration. Steal the body, and they'd want the box and the finger back where they could guard it closely. And who better to trust with its safe return to the Embassy than their most accomplished Undoer.' He thrust out his jaw and smiled tightly, clearly feeling very pleased with himself. Jake was flicking nervous glances at the stairs. Hoping someone, anyone, would come.

'Except Stiffkey gave it to me . . .' said Jake, goading Goodmourning to keep speaking.

'Yes, you rather ruined that part of the plan, kid!' he said, slapping Jake hard on the back. 'But anyway! Here we all are, so no harm done, eh? And no hard feelings, I hope?' He ruffled Jake's hair then grabbed a fistful, forcing him forward and downwards until he was on his knees at the grave's edge.

'You'll want to see this properly, I'm sure,' said Goodmourning.

Inside the grave was an open lead-lined coffin, and inside that, sunken eyed and withered, still dressed in the remnants of his silken pyjamas, was the corpse of Dasaev, the composer – the poor man who had let his body be occupied by the spirit of a fallen reaper.

Goodmourning let go of Jake's hair and he fell forward, frantically scrabbling back from the edge of the freshly dug grave.

The finger in his hoodie pocket was wriggling wildly now, sensing the proximity of the body it desperately wanted to be united with. Jake's free hand clamped down on his pocket to prevent it jumping out. Again, he flicked a desperate look at the doorway. Surely Mawkins or the Ambassador or someone would be on their way?!

'And now . . .' said Goodmourning majestically, 'IT IS TIME!'

He placed Cora's trophy on the floor behind him and knelt at the foot of the grave, cradling the box like it was newborn kitten, his fingers stroking the lid tenderly.

Jake looked to where the trophy stood. If he could just reach it . . .

Goodmourning was now carefully unlatching the hook of the box and gently opening the lid, too engrossed in the box's contents to notice Jake slowly edging closer. The box started to vibrate.

'It moves within its bedding!' Goodmourning whispered in excitement, his voice changing in tone. 'His spirit is present and yearns to be united with his body!'

Slowly and carefully his fingers moved the newspaper aside. One fragment at a time. The vibrating was louder now. Rhythmic and mechanical. Goodmourning frowned and, reaching into the box, pulled out not a finger, but Jake's mobile phone. His face twisted in anger and confusion.

He turned the phone round in his fingers. A light was flashing on the screen and the word MUM could be read.

'Where is my finger?' he said in a low, menacing voice.

In the otherwise tense silence of the mausoleum, a voice could be heard, distant and tinny: Jake's mum.

'Jake? Are you there? Why haven't you been answering your phone? I've been worried sick!'

And that's when things went crazy.

THE ARRIVAL

Goodmourning hurled down the phone and turned to Jake, just as Jake's fingers reached Cora's trophy.

'WHERE IS THE FINGER?!' Goodmourning shouted at full volume. He opened a palm and Jake felt his body jerk backwards, pressed against the wall of the tomb, held there by an invisible force. His hand that held the trophy was pinned to the wall. Jake turned the trophy in his fingers until it was upside down then prised the lid open with his thumb. Cora materialised next to Goodmourning with an expression of pure rage, her hockey stick ready to strike.

'I'll show you what happens to people who close my lid!' she screamed at Goodmourning, and swung the hockey stick with all her might. The stick passed a hair's breadth from Goodmourning's face, as he lurched backwards to avoid the blow. It was enough to break his concentration. Jake slid down the wall gasping for breath.

Jake's mum's voice rose up from the phone again. 'Are you having fun, Jake?'

Cora looked at Jake. 'You're kidding me, right?'

'Who's that, Jake?' said Mum.

It was Stiffkey's turn to move into action now. Before Goodmourning could gather himself, he swung his shovel at his head, making solid contact that echoed with a dull clang around the mausoleum. Goodmourning staggered backwards, blood pouring from his nose, and stepped on the phone. He sank to the ground with his face in his hands. Jake crawled forward and grabbed the phone. 'It's OK. It's not broken!' he announced.

Cora stalked towards Goodmourning, who was picking himself up off the ground, her hockey stick raised and ready for action. 'I'll teach you to touch my trophy!'

'Is that your girlfriend, Jake?' came Mum's tinny voice.

'Mum!' said Jake, going red. 'I'll call you later, OK?' He hung up the phone and shoved it in his jeans pocket.

Goodmourning raised his hand again as Cora advanced on him, but this time the incantation was different. Cora's trophy rolled on the ground then sprang into his hand as though drawn by a terrible magnet. Just as her stick was about to make contact, he flipped the lid shut.

'You—!' she shouted, as she was sucked back into the trophy before she could swear properly. Goodmourning sneered and spat blood on to the dirt floor.

Jake sprang up, preparing to leap at Goodmourning. He felt something fall from his pocket and heard Stiffkey cry out with shock. 'Heaven preserve us! The Damned Thing is loose!'

Jake clapped his hand to his pocket. *The finger was gone.* His eyes darted to where Stiffkey was pointing.

There on the floor, only a matter of inches from the edge of the grave, was the finger. It bent at the knuckle, drawing its stump towards its fingernail, forming itself into an arch, then letting gravity take hold and topple it over. It was moving fast, now mere inches from the grave.

'The finger has found its master!' cried Goodmourning. 'The reign of Fenris will begin!'

Jake launched himself towards the finger but it was too late. The Damned Thing had made it to the edge and, with one last writhing motion, it toppled into the grave. 'No!' shrieked Jake.

There was a blur of fur and teeth. Jake watched as a shimmering shape flew down the stairs and leaped into the grave.

'Zorro!' cried Jake, as the brave fox landed on the chest of the composer, caught the finger in his jaws, then bounded from the grave in one fluid movement. He dropped the finger into Jake's hand.

Jake looked across the mausoleum. To his horror he saw that Goodmourning had released Cora and was holding her round the neck. Cora struggled against his grip but it was no use. His magic was too strong.

Goodmourning smiled. 'I think it's rather apt that you should be the one to reunite the composer with his finger. Otherwise I shall have to hurt your little friend here.'

'I'm already dead – there's nothing you can do to me! Ignore him, Jake, don't do it!' she shouted.

'Well, it's true I can't kill you, but I could always send you to the Void. Do you like eternal pain?' Goodmourning sneered at his powerless victim.

'You wouldn't know how,' said Stiffkey. 'Only a reaper has that sort of power.'

'Can you be so sure?' said Goodmourning. 'It's surprising, the reach of Old Magic, once it has been mastered.'

Cora had tears in her eyes. 'Don't do it, Jake. Don't do what he wants.'

Suddenly, Jake smiled. 'Don't worry, Cora. Everything's going to be fine.'

Everyone frowned in confusion. Jake no doubt seemed calm. Strangely calm for someone who was about to be forced to slot the last piece of an evil jigsaw into place and bring about the downfall of the Earthly Plane.

But he was calm for a reason. He had seen something. Something behind Goodmourning.

Something that had been creeping down the stairs and had now begun to swirl around their feet. Goodmourning looked over his shoulder. His grip on Cora's neck loosened and she dropped to the dirt.

The mausoleum was filling with fog.

At the top of the stairs stood Mawkins.

THE TALKING HARE

Mawkins descended the stairs. The fog that licked out from beneath his robes dispersed in his wake and gathered in the corners of the stone chamber.

Seen close up and in an enclosed space he was even more forbidding. He was so tall that his head almost touched the ceiling and he towered over them all, his face still unseeable in the utter shadow of his hood.

The room waited, everyone in it too terrified to move.

The dead hare around Mawkins' neck twitched. With a sudden jerk of its head its milky eyes flicked open. Then, to Jake's horror, it opened its mouth and began to speak.

Though Jake could understand the meaning of

the words, the voice that rattled from the hare's mouth wasn't of this world.

'Where. Is. The. Finger.'

It took Jake a moment to compose himself and find his own voice again.

He stepped forward. 'It's here.' He held out the wriggling finger on a flat palm.

'It's mine!' screamed Goodmourning. He lurched forward then stopped suddenly at the sound of a new voice from the top of the stairs.

'Actually, I think that item is the property of the Embassy of the Dead.'

Three ghosts stood at the top of the steps.

A woman in jodhpurs and a riding hat entered the chamber and stood sternly with her hands on her hips and a frown on her face. Behind her stood a man in blood stained military clothes and an officious-looking woman in glasses holding a clipboard.

'Ambassador!' said Goodmourning, with a huge smile on his face. Then, looking at the man, 'Captain.' He ran a hand nervously through his hair. 'I'm glad you're both here at last to sort this mess—'

'Button it,' said the Ambassador.

The woman with the clipboard bustled her way to the front. 'Which one of you is Jake Green?' she asked.

'I am,' said Jake, sheepishly.

'I believe we spoke earlier? My name is Maureen Perkins, personal assistant to the Ambassador.'

Jake nodded dumbly.

'I've a section 7.3b Death Order here with your name on it,' she said. She looked over at Stiffkey. 'And Albert Stiffkey, ghost?'

Stiffkey nodded, grimly. 'Aye, that's me, but the boy ain't nothing to do with this business. It's my fault and my fault alone.'

Maureen tutted. 'An unfortunate business indeed. It's always a shame to send a living child to the Eternal Void. Still, rules are rules . . .' Here Maureen paused for a moment, got a tissue from her pocket, and blew her nose. She looked up again. 'Could I have the finger, please.' Jake went to pass it to her.

'Goodness, no! In the box, child. I don't want to touch it!'

Cora picked up the box and Jake replaced the finger. He looked at Goodmourning, whose expression was unreadable. Clearly he was outnumbered, but he was also desperate and might try anything.

Jake carefully closed the lid and handed the box to Maureen, who passed it to the Ambassador.

'We've been following the situation for a while, Goodmourning,' said the Ambassador, 'wondering why you hadn't called us in, but thanks to Jake alerting us, I think we do now have the full picture. It seems you've betrayed us and have been plotting to free Fenris, with no regard for the danger that poses to both the Earthly Plane and the Afterworld.'

'Absolutely not! I've simply been—'

'Enough!' boomed the Ambassador, and the mausoleum seemed to shake at her voice. 'The game is up, Goodmourning. I'm afraid your man, Rayburn – as insensitive as he is to the presence of ghosts – turned out to be quite talkative when faced with the Captain.'

The Captain smiled. 'I'm afraid, Goodmourning, your time at the Embassy is over.'

'Well, *I'm* afraid it's too late to stop me now!' shouted Goodmourning. He held his open palms out towards Mawkins and uttered an incantation. Nothing happened.

Mawkins took a step towards Goodmourning.

'N-no, wait, that's not it!' Goodmourning stuttered and tried the chant again, stumbling on his words.

Maureen began reading from her clipboard.

'Section 56.c: Unauthorised use of incantations and Old Magic,' she said.

Mawkins took another step forward.

'Section 45.c: Activities pertaining or belonging to an organisation and/or person actively involved in overthrowing the Embassy.'

And another.

'Section 24.5.1: Harming a member of the living. Subsection 12: Attempted murder.'

She shook her head crossly. 'Really, Undoer Goodmourning. You've racked up an impressive tally of infringements. I'd say I've got more than enough evidence to proceed without further paperwork. Mawkins, if you would be so kind?'

A terrified Goodmourning was now backed against the wall as Mawkins advanced on him. The sucking Void between Mawkins' hands was picking up pace now.

'No, wait, please . . .'

The dead hare scratched its whiskers with its paw. 'Goodbye.'

Mawkins raised his hands and then, with a sudden swinging movement, his scythe appeared and sliced a deep cut in the air. Jake could only stare into the eternal blackness. A void that continued forever. A cry grabbed his attention back to his own side of the cut. Goodmourning was being dragged towards the hole. He stumbled, fingernails raking the dirt floor of the mausoleum.

'No!' He pleaded. 'Not this. Not the Eternal Void!'

His hand reached out for Jake's ankle, but Stiffkey batted it away with his shovel. Goodmourning lost his purchase on the soil and was sucked into the hole. Mawkins waved a hand and the cut in the air healed.

Stiffkey took off his hat and lowered his head. 'There ain't no one that deserves the Void . . . Not even mister Goodmourning.'

Maureen tore a sheet from her clipboard and held it out for Stiffkey to take. 'But we must do things according to the letter of the law, mustn't we?'

Stiffkey nodded grimly, taking the sheet and folding it neatly. 'Aye, that we must, Mrs Perkins.'

'Ms,' she corrected. 'Albert Stiffkey. This certificate authorises me to send you to the Eternal Void. Do you accept your fate?'

Mawkins turned towards the ghost, raising his hands to summon his scythe.

'That's not fair!' shouted Cora.

'Well, Ms Sanderford, as you well know, life isn't always fair, but we must abide by the rules,' said

Maureen gently but firmly. 'And as you have had unauthorised contact with an unlicenced member of the living, you have barely escaped the Void yourself. It's only because you are a Possessor, tied to your trophy, and technically you were summoned, that your presence here is not entirely your own fault. Goodness knows how Ezekiel got that so wrong . . .' She shook her head, making a note on her clipboard.

'Thank you,' said Cora, 'but it's still not fair . . . Jake . . . Stiffkey . . . they really were trying to do the right thing.'

Stiffkey stepped forward. 'It's all right, child, Ms Perkins be right. Rules are rules and I be acceptin' of my fate and only hope the Eternal Void ain't worse than the eternal longings.' He frowned and reached a long arm towards Jake. Some dirt fell from his jacket sleeve and gathered in a heap at Jake's feet. 'But if this young lad is to be sent to the Void for my mistakes then them rules ain't worth the paper they be written on.'

Maureen shook her head. 'I'm afraid the time to register an appeal to a Death Order has passed.

You would have needed to have handed in form AQ23 within twenty-four hours of the Death Order being issued.'

Now Jake stepped forward. Something Mr Sixsmith had said in the Afterworld reverberated around his head. *If he shops you and you go to the Void first then he's not in trouble any more.*

'Wait!' shouted Jake. 'The only reason you're sending Stiffkey to the Void is because he's in contact with an unlicensed member of the living: me, right?'

'That is correct,' replied Maureen.

'And so if you send me to the Void first I'll no longer be living and he'll be pardoned?' Jake wracked his brain for the final detail in his conversation with Mr Sixsmith, then remembered. 'Subsection c, I believe?'

Maureen frowned, then flicked through the pages on her clipboard. 'Well, it's been a while since Subsection c has been invoked – in fact I'm not sure that it ever has, but . . . you are correct.'

Jake stepped between the two ghosts. 'Then send me to the Void first,' he pleaded. He looked up at his old friend. 'Better one of us go than both.'

Stiffkey started as though he'd been struck by lightning. 'No! I won't let it happen, boy!'

Maureen sighed. 'Well, let's get it over with then. If you'd like to go first, Mr Stiffkey.'

Stiffkey nodded. 'If I might just be allowed a moment . . .' he said, clearing his throat. 'I've already lost a son – and I never got to tell him how I felt before I died – not really. Us undertakers ain't good at showing their feelings. And Jake, though you ain't my true son, I love you like you were.' He smiled sadly at Jake. 'I'm glad at least to be able to do it right this time and tell you before I be going on my way.'

'Very touching,' said Maureen, looking up from her clipboard. 'Will that be all?'

Stiffkey nodded and closed his eyes in preparation.

But as Mawkins took a step towards him and the scythe hovered ominously in the air, a sudden thought struck Jake.

'Stiffkey, did you never tell your son you loved him?' he said.

'No, boy, I didn't,' said the ghost, shaking his head.

'Say it now, Stiffkey!' said Jake excitedly. 'Say it out loud! Shout it! Go on!'

And Stiffkey looked down at him, at once knowing what Jake meant. His eyes lit up. He took off his top hat and brushed some dirt from the rim. And now tears were streaming down his face. He raised his arms, looked up at the ceiling and shouted, 'I love you, Sidney! I love you, my son!'

And just as the Void was about to consume him, Stiffkey began to fade. Not from the extremities. Not from his top hat, nor his fingers, nor his feet, but from the middle – his heart.

'What's happening?' said Cora in a hushed voice.

Mawkins lowered his hands. The Void disappeared.

'He's been Undone,' said Jake, tears falling down his own cheeks.

Stiffkey's eyes flicked open and a huge smile spread across his face – a look of pure childlike joy. 'I'm off to see my boy! You did it, Jake. You've untied the Gordian knot. Thank you. You've saved us both!'

Jake blinked and Stiffkey held out a fading hand towards him. 'You be an Undoer now, boy. Good luck! And goodbye.'

'Goodbye, Stiffkey!' said Jake, reaching out for his friend's hand, but where their fingers should've met, now his hand passed through air. Albert Stiffkey had left the Earthly Plane for ever.

Maureen shrugged and tucked her clipboard beneath her arm. 'Well, that's that, then. You're an Undoer, and the 7.3 Death Order is invalidated as you are now licenced.'

She seemed a little put out.

Jake and Cora looked at each other and broke into huge smiles. She ran over to him and they hugged and jumped up and down.

'You did it!' said Cora. 'You really did it!'

'Not so fast,' came a stern voice.

Jake and Cora stopped and turned. It was the Ambassador, still standing hand on hip. She was eyeing Jake steadily.

'You have just managed to Undo Stiffkey and, given you have also managed to ensure the safe return of the finger, that does seem to be enough in this instance to save you from the Eternal Void.'

Jake smiled and nodded gratefully. 'Thank you, Ambassador.'

'BUT,' she went on, raising a finger, 'you are not out of trouble yet. You have still led the Embassy on a wild goose chase across the country, all the time meddling in the affairs of the dead.'

She wagged her finger at him. 'All with the intention of saving your own skin. Yet had you been able to think about anything other than yourself, you might have considered that the entire Earthly Plane and all its inhabitants were in the gravest danger.'

Jake shuffled on his feet. 'Any honourable person would have known that the only correct course of action would have been to report IMMEDIATELY to the Embassy and deliver the finger back to safety.'

Cora went to say something but a glare from the Ambassador was enough to silence her.

'Have you stopped to consider what would have happened if we had arrived a moment later?'

Jake stood there speechless, unable to say anything.

'You may have qualified for an Undoer's licence, but there's a reason why the Embassy hasn't ever employed a living child before. A child's inability to see beyond their own existence on the Earthly Plane never ceases to disappoint.' She pursed her lips. 'I'm very much hoping I won't see you again. At least not until you're dead. Now go home.' And with a click of her fingers, the Ambassador, the Captain and Maureen Perkins all disappeared.

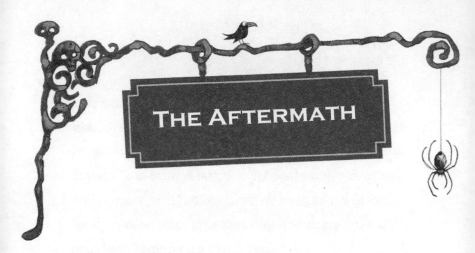

THE AFTERMATH

'It's probably not as grand as the Sanderford estate, or even the dinner hall at Bodelean's,' said Jake as he opened the front door to his house. 'But at least we have proper ketchup!'

Cora pulled a face. 'It'll do, I suppose.' Jake looked a little hurt and she shoved him. 'I'm kidding! It's lovely. Don't be so sensitive.'

Jake had smiled at the thought of Cora haunting his mum's tiny spare bedroom, and Zorro the space under his bed. He was excited to at last be able to have a pet, even if it was a dead one.

Jake removed his shoes and put his rucksack down on the floor.

'Is that you, love?' came an excited and familiar voice.

Cora looked at him and nodded.

Quickly, Jake closed the lid of the trophy and she disappeared. He popped it into his bag as his mum came tearing towards him.

'Jake! You're back! I've missed you.' She grabbed his cheeks and gave him a big kiss. He was glad that Cora was safely hidden away. 'Your dad's coming round soon. He wanted to be here when you got back, but he said there was a problem with the campervan. Some joyriders stole it, then returned it covered in mud and with a dead crow in the glove compartment!'

Jake held back a smile and tried to look shocked.

His mum gathered him up in her arms. 'It's good to have you home! I love you,' she said.

Jake looked up at her, so pleased to be home. Then he thought of Dad, still living on the farm, and felt sad again.

There was a knock on the door.

Mum reluctantly untangled her arms from around Jake and opened the door.

Dad was standing there, sweating slightly. 'Hi Jake,' said Dad, his eyes twinkling. 'How was the trip?'

Jake shrugged. 'Fine, I suppose.' He turned and padded up the stairs with his rucksack. 'I'm just going to have a shower, I'll be down in a bit.'

'OK,' said Mum, in a voice that sounded sad.

Jake stopped halfway up the stairs and looked back. 'Mum, Dad?'

'Yes?' they said together, staring up at him.

'I love you.'

ONE WEEK LATER

'Jake! You're going to miss the school bus!'

'Coming, Mum!' he said.

Jake looked down at the chessboard. It didn't matter where he moved his queen - she would be taken. He pulled a face. Then he knocked his king over.

Cora smiled. '7-0!'

For someone who was so keen on experiencing new things, she never seemed to get bored of winning. Though, to be honest, once you'd been chased across the country by the grimmest of grim reapers everything else felt a bit dull. Jake wouldn't admit it out loud, but deep down, he kind of missed the thrill of it all. Safety felt a little boring now.

The door opened and Mum's head poked

through. 'I've got to go. Do you need a lift to the bus stop?'

'Doesn't she ever knock, Precious?' asked Cora.

Jake ignored the question and checked the time on his phone. 'No, I'll walk, Mum, it's a nice day.'

'OK, love, I'll see you tonight. Something arrived for you . . .'

She held out a dog-eared postcard. 'It came through the post today. I'd have assumed it had got stuck in the post office for fifty years by the look of it – but it's addressed to you.'

Jake turned it over in his hands. On one side was a sepia picture of some old manor house, and on the other his name and address written in neat handwriting. There was no message.

His mum shrugged and left the room.

'What is it?' asked Cora, eager to see.

'A postcard . . .' he said thoughtfully. Then he recognised the manor house. He'd only seen it at night before, and in its current form – a crumbling ruin.

'Wistman's Lodge!' breathed Cora, reading his mind. 'It's from the Embassy! What does it say?'

Jake turned it over to show her the blank side.

'Nothing . . .' he said, then paused, the words of an old friend whispering through his memory . . .

Us ghosts and the things us ghosts like to hide are made of exactly that. Nothingness . . .

Jake looked again at the postcard in a not-looking-at-anything-in-particular sort of way, and words started to appear, in neat copperplate handwriting, scratched lightly into the yellowing cardboard.

His eyes grew wide.

'We've been summoned!'

ACKNOWLEDGEMENTS

In Memorandum

Thanks to:
Samantha Swinnerton, who dug the plot
(and also to Lily Morgan, who helped fill it in).

Thanks to:
Orion Children's Books, especially: Ruth Alltimes,
Naomi Berwin, Katy Cattell, Valentina Fazio, Nicola Goode,
Helen Hughes, Dom Kingston, Hilary Murray Hill,
Tom Sanderson, Andrew Sharp, Sophie Stericker
and Lucy Upton. Whether you paid for the flowers,
carried the coffin or informed the neighbours what the
strange smell was, your help was greatly appreciated.

Thanks to:
Ben for being there at the beginning
and Richard for being there at the end.
Jonty and Tilly for the readings.
Paul, for making sure I got my fair share of
sausage rolls at the wake.

And also to:
Chris Mould, for making the corpse presentable.

W ill Mabbitt has an overactive imagination. It used to get him in trouble, but now it's his job. His first book, *The Unlikely Adventures of Mabel Jones*, was shortlisted for the Branford Boase Award. He's achieved little of else note, preferring to spend his time loitering in graveyards looking for ideas. He lives with his family on the south coast of England.

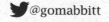 @gomabbitt

Watch out for more

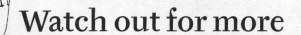

EMBASSY OF THE DEAD

COMING SOON!*

*Will contain even more
spooky spectres,
grave matters
and near-death encounters.